"Muerto!"

Slowly the massive bulk of the man tipped forward over the rock, across the trail and into the canyon. Owl had the satisfaction of looking directly into the face of El Gato. At only a little more than arm's length, he saw the brutal, sadistic expression change to one of stark terror.

El Gato did not scream. There was only a short choking gasp of disbelief as he launched into the void. He spread his arms wide, grasping at nothingness, and seemed to hover like an eagle when she leaves her nest. Then he plummeted downward.

Owl crouched on the narrow shelf, watching the man's body disappear among the fir tips far below.

"Run!" shouted Long Bow. "El Gato is dead!"

Prisoners began to scatter up the slope, and owl darted around the rock and joined in the escape. . . .

ALSO BY DON COLDSMITH

The Elk-Dog Heritage
Buffalo Medicine
Daughter of the Eagle
The Long Journey Home

DON COLDSMITH

BUFFALO MEDICINE

A TOM DOHERTY ASSOCIATES BOOK
NEW YORK

This is a work of fiction. All the characters and events portrayed in this book are either products of the author's imagination or are used fictitiously.

BUFFALO MEDICINE

Copyright © 1981 by Don Coldsmith

Previously published by Doubleday Books in 1981

A Forge Book
Published by Tom Doherty Associates, LLC
175 Fifth Avenue
New York, NY 10010

www.tor.com

Forge® is a registered trademark of Tom Doherty Associates, LLC.

ISBN: 0-812-57969-0
EAN 975-0812-57969-7

First edition: December 2003
First mass market edition: December 2004

Printed in the United States of America

0 9 8 7 6 5 4 3 2 1

BUFFALO

MEDICINE

1

Owl sat on a limestone outcropping near the crest of a hill overlooking the village. The rolling prairie spread before him, green in the Moon of Grass-growing. Darker green slashes marked the course of wandering streams. Clumps of willow contrasted in lighter tones with the deeper hues of the hardwoods.

Beneath the boy's position were scattered the lodges of the Elk-dog band of the People. There was the usual noise, barking of countless dogs, and the buzzing activity of large numbers of people living in close proximity. In all, it was a peaceful scene, but Owl was not in a mood to appreciate it. He was troubled.

Through all his twelve summers, Owl had realized that he was different from other children. His mother, the Tall One, had told him this from the time he could remember. He wasn't certain what the difference was. Certainly, he was the son of a chief, but it was more than that. Owl and his older brother, Eagle, were regarded somehow as special by the People. Most of the other children seemed to regard them with awe and respect.

There were a few exceptions, and one of these was the cause of his current depression. Two Dogs, slightly older, taller, and stronger, had increasingly made Owl's life miserable. The boy rubbed his bruised shoulder, and gently touched a skinned spot on his knee. It was beyond his understanding that Two Dogs had initiated the fight. It had not been one of the good-natured contests constantly carried out by the youths of the Rabbit Society. The other's attitude had been one of resentment and hostility.

Then there was Two Dogs' remark, which had finally caused Owl to attack in a blind rage. "You think you are special because your father has fur upon his face."

It was true. Heads Off, the chief, was the only man Owl had ever seen with facial hair. But again, it was apparently regarded with awe and respect by most of the People. Tall One eagerly examined the face of Eagle from time to time, proudly pointing out the new growth of fuzz along his upper lip and jaw. Yet there was the undercurrent of resentment by the occasional malcontent like Two Dogs.

Owl had attempted to discuss this situation with Eagle. His brother was inclined to shrug the matter aside.

"It is nothing, Owl. Our father is a chief, and a good one. Two Dogs would rather be a chief's son than a nobody."

The father of Two Dogs was certainly a nobody. The family was constantly living on the brink of poverty because of his addiction to gambling. Perhaps this was part of the cause of Two Dogs' bitterness, thought Owl.

None of this seemed to bother Eagle in the least. He was a happy, well-liked youth, tall and strong, and able to glory in his skills. He was an able horseman, capable with the bow and the lance. In wrestling, he could best any of the

Rabbit Society, and many of the adults. It was acknowledged that his leadership abilities would make him an excellent chief to eventually succeed his father.

Eagle was, in short, not the sort to be the object of a bully's attentions. Consequently, Two Dogs had turned his attention to the chief's younger son.

Owl did not lack in physical ability. His skill in hunting rabbits with the throwing sticks was well known. He had displayed himself well in the fight just past. But still, he preferred to think rather than fight, if it came to a choice. And why, he desperately wondered, did Two Dogs hate him? What was it that was different, that Owl did not understand?

Still depressed, he rose with a sigh and started down the hill, hitching up the thong that held his breech-clout in place. He would go and talk to his grandfather, who would surely understand. Coyote could always be relied on to bring comfort, a smile, and perhaps some valuable advice. And, he was much more approachable than Owl's father, the chief.

The boy threaded his way among the conical lodges. He paused only to kick irritably at a barking dog and to send a well-aimed rock after the retreating animal.

Coyote was seated in front of the lodge, propped comfortably against his willow back rest. Pungent smoke drifted from his pipe as he complacently observed the village. His bright eyes flickered everywhere, overlooking nothing, though his demeanor was one of complete relaxation.

"Uncle," began Owl, using the term of address for any adult male of the People, "I would speak with you."

Coyote motioned to the grass beside him and nodded. Owl sank to the squatting position of rest and waited. It was a thing of good manners to wait now until invited to speak. His grandfather did not force him to wait long.

"Yes, my son," he inquired, "you are troubled?"

Owl blurted out his story, nearly in tears. "Tell me, Grandfather, what is it?" he finished.

Coyote took three long puffs on his stone pipe before he spoke. Finally he knocked the dottle into his palm and tossed the ashes to the ground. He rose to his feet, placing the pipe on his willow rest.

"Owl, my son, come with me. I think it is time for you to have a visit with White Buffalo."

Apprehension gripped the boy. White Buffalo, the medicine man, was universally respected by the People, but also feared by the youngsters. He was very old, probably more than fifty winters, Owl thought. His wrinkled face had a perpetual look of stern disapproval, almost a scowl. True, Owl could not remember any one who had actually been harmed by the medicine man. His medicine, however, was assumed to be very powerful. In any major tribal decision, the chiefs, even Owl's father, were dependent on White Buffalo's visions. The children at play would frighten each other with threats of the wrath of White Buffalo, and speak in hushed whispers of his spells and incantations.

Thus, Owl's heart beat faster and he found it difficult to swallow as they approached the lodge of the medicine man. Coyote paused outside the brightly decorated structure and called out to announce their presence. An old woman, wife of the medicine man, Owl knew, drew aside the hanging skin of the doorway, and beckoned the visitors inside.

"*Ah-koh*, Uncle," began Coyote. Owl knew that the two men were close friends, though White Buffalo was much the older. "I have brought Owl to speak with you."

The old man nodded, and wonder of wonders, almost smiled. His eyes narrowed to wrinkled slits as he peered at the boy. He motioned them to seats on the robes beside him.

"Yes, boy," he growled, "what do you want?"

Owl, nearly shaking in his moccasins, could not answer. In this moment of stress, if he had been asked his own name he probably would have missed the correct answer. He gulped a time or two and attempted to phrase his problem, unsuccessfully. At last he was rescued by his grandfather.

"This young man, Uncle, is troubled. Owl feels that somehow he is different from other youths of the People. This makes Owl very unhappy. I have thought perhaps you might speak of these things to this young man."

White Buffalo stared piercingly at his young visitor for a long moment before he answered. Then he nodded.

"So it will be."

The old man turned and reached into the storage space under the lodge lining behind him. He brought forth several tightly rolled skins, examined them briefly, and selected one. The others were returned to their place.

Owl was immediately impressed with the reverence the medicine man exhibited for the object in his hands. The gnarled old fingers untied the thongs that held the roll in place. His hands started very carefully to unroll the soft-tanned buckskin. Suddenly Owl realized what the roll contained. It could be only one thing. He was to be allowed to view one of the precious Story Skins, on which were recorded the history of the People.

"You know, my son, what this is?" White Buffalo was asking as he ceremoniously unrolled the skin.

Owl only nodded, wide-eyed and unable to speak. The old man spread the skin before them. Dozens of small pictographic figures showed plainly in the dim light of the lodge.

"The story starts in the center," White Buffalo continued, "and circles outward. One picture is added each summer, showing the most important thing that has come to be for the People. Ah, here it is!"

He seemed to have been looking for something, and now pointed to one of the story pictures. It was upside down to Owl, being at the far side of the skin. He could see, however, that it was a picture of a man on a horse.

"Many summers ago, before you were born, my son, the People had no elk-dogs. All the hunting was done on foot. Sometimes the hunt was poor, and the People were hungry. Sometimes we starved." He pointed to an earlier picture, with emaciated figures and burial scaffolds for the dead.

"Then your father, Heads Off, came among us, with his elk-dog."

Owl had, of course, heard this story before, from the time of his birth. He had become tired and bored with it. Yet, with the story pictures in front of him, a new dimension was added. He eagerly looked more closely at the skin. Yes, on the face of the mounted figure there was hair. It was his father. Eagerly, the boy looked ahead. Some of the scenes resembled those of the lodge lining in his father's lodge. There were scenes depicting a successful buffalo hunt, and combat with the dreaded Head Splitters. The Great Battle, with both groups mounted on horses for the first time, was one of the biggest events in the recent history of the People. A resounding victory had resulted, though the chief of the Southern band had been killed. Yes, there was the dead chief, and Owl's father taking over the position. That had been the year before Owl's birth. Eagle had been only a baby.

There were other events, too, which Owl had never seen depicted before, though he had heard them mentioned. The Big Winter, when Sun Boy's torch had almost gone out. And the death of four young men of the People, who had ventured out ill-advised and encountered a band of Head Splitters. Owl began to regard, with a special kind of awe, the medicine man, custodian of all this fascinating information. That individual was still talking, retelling the stories in a singsong sort of chant.

"—and so, since the coming of the elk-dog, it has been easier to kill buffalo. The People have full bellies, and many robes for warmth. It was good when Heads Off, the mighty hunter, came to us with his elk-dog medicine."

Although he had heard this story before, Owl suddenly began to grasp a part of the situation he had always ignored. "Heads Off brought us the elk-dogs" was the familiar phrasing of the tale. But now, for Owl, there was something missing.

"Uncle," he began eagerly, almost interrupting the old man. "You must know—where did my father come *from* to the People?"

Coyote, quietly lounging in the shadows, was pleased. His grandson had hit upon the crux of the situation. Coyote nodded to himself. This boy would be a worthy one to bear the blood of the family.

"My son," the medicine man was speaking, "Heads Off came from a place far beyond the Big Water. None of the People has ever been there. Your father was never able to return to his own tribe."

This, thought Owl, is why I feel different. I *am* different. His head was swimming with the sudden realization that he had never stopped to consider before.

"Then," he muttered, half to himself, "my father is not even of the People."

"No," agreed the old man, reading correctly the boy's downcast expression. It would be quite a blow to discover that one was an outsider, especially at twelve summers. "No, but Heads Off is well honored by the People. They have made him chief. He is now one of us."

Owl still looked dubious. In the back of his mind was forming an ambition. Some day he would go and find his father's tribe.

"Of course," continued White Buffalo, "there are always a few who resent the success of others. But your father has earned his honors. His medicine is very powerful. As strong as my own, in a different way."

This was a favorite topic of the old medicine man. He warmed to his subject.

"Mine is the medicine of the buffalo. My visions tell the People where to hunt, and how to find the herds. Your father's medicine is that of the elk-dog. With this medicine, he controls the elk-dogs, so that men ride upon them to hunt or to fight."

He pointed to one of the later pictures. The chief, in ceremonial dress, wore on his chest the symbol of his medicine. The iron bit for the horse's mouth, brought from across the Big Water. Owl had seen it many times, hanging in its place of honor over his father's bed. It was no longer used in a horse's mouth. It had become symbolic of control over the elk-dogs. An object not to be used, but worn only ceremonially, and honored.

But, in the mind of a youth of twelve, that which is familiar is never so exciting as that which is unknown.

"Tell me, Uncle, how do you learn where to find the buffalo?"

It was a more complicated question than it appeared. Implied in the query was a genuine interest in all the medicine involved. It could not be answered simply. The old man waited a long time before answering. How could he sum up in a few words the years of experience required? How could the boy grasp the intricate knowledge of the prairie, the interdependence of the teeming life on the plains? One had to know exactly when to fire the prairie in the Moon of Grass-growing, to bring the buffalo back. All this in addition to judgment. The chiefs relied heavily on the visions of the medicine man. White Buffalo shrugged.

"The visions, of course."

He was feeling a little depressed as he talked with this boy. The old man had been concerned about who would take over his responsibilities. He increasingly felt the encroachment of age and infirmity, and he had no apprentice. The usual candidate would have been his son, but he and his wife had never had a child. *Aiee,* what a disappointment.

For years now, he had looked for a young man to be his understudy. Several had seemed good possibilities. Coyote, for one, but each had selected other pursuits. In recent years, there had been almost no interest on the part of any of the young men. They were all too busy with learning the use of the elk-dogs and the real-spear.

If White Buffalo had known the thoughts of his young guest, he would have felt considerably more cheerful. Owl's head was full of thrilling thoughts of the Story Skins, of buffalo medicine, and of all the knowledge in the mind of the medicine man. He struggled with these thoughts a long time. If he were to grow up not quite fitting the pattern of the other boys, maybe he could fit into this type of activity. Hesitantly, he spoke.

"Uncle, how does one become a medicine man?"

White Buffalo was overwhelmed, but managed to conceal his elation. His grim countenance became even more grim.

"Come back tomorrow," he growled. "We will talk."

Neither Owl nor his grandfather spoke as they wound their way back toward the lodge of the boy's parents. Coyote, however, smiled quietly to himself. He had seen the increasing moodiness of young Owl, who appeared to be a thinker.

Sometimes, Coyote mused, it needs only to bring the right ones together at the right time. He was very pleased with his afternoon's accomplishment.

2

Owl spent a restless night. The excitement of the coming day kept him tossing and dreaming. During his more coherent moments, between fitful sleep, he somehow felt that he was about to discover all the secrets of existence.

At the appointed hour, Owl presented himself before the lodge of White Buffalo, and called out his presence. The old woman smiled and beckoned him inside. He could feel his heart beating rapidly as he stood before the medicine man. White Buffalo, grim and scowling as ever, motioned him to sit. After a long pause, the old man began to speak.

"I have searched for a vision, my son. I have seen shadows of things to come." The piercing old eyes seemed to bore completely through the boy. Owl felt that the medicine man was examining his very spirit, the secret part where he lived, hidden from all others. The boy repressed a sudden urge to retreat, to escape from the powerful presence of the old man.

"You will travel far, and see strong medicines," the hypnotic, droning voice continued. "You will find the tribe of your father."

Owl was startled. Did the medicine man know that he only yesterday had formed that ambition?

"You can become a great medicine man," White Buffalo went on, "but the trail is steep and rocky." He paused a long time. "Are you ready for the hard work that is needed?"

Owl nodded eagerly. "Yes, Uncle, I have thought much of this through the night. I am ready."

By evening, the entire village was aware that Owl had apprenticed himself to the medicine man. His parents were pleased and encouraging. Owl had decided not to mention his quest for his father's tribe, or White Buffalo's strange vision concerning it.

Eagle was interested, but primarily curious, as an older brother inquiring about the activities of the younger.

Coyote found occasion to draw his grandson aside to congratulate him.

"You have chosen well, my son. There are few men who could teach you as much as White Buffalo. He would not take you as his helper unless he saw your strength and wisdom. But it will be hard!"

The boys of Owl's own age were overawed at the step he had taken. Most were congratulatory, but some were true to form.

"Owl still thinks he is better than others," scoffed Two Dogs. His envy now seemed to be more biting than ever. He attempted to start trouble repeatedly, but Owl resisted all taunts. Somehow, it would not seem appropriate for the medicine man's assistant to be brawling in the dirt like other youths.

Besides, Owl found immediately, he had very little

time for frivolous pursuits. He was kept busy helping White Buffalo with the implements of his profession. Owl carried and fetched, helped to dig roots, pick leaves, flowers, and seeds of various herbs, and prepare them for storage. At the same time he was required to learn identification and use, and how to look for likely spots where the desired plants might grow.

Sometimes, for no apparent reason, White Buffalo would rouse his young assistant at odd hours. The two would climb the hills, Owl laboring under the load of the medicine man's pack. He would sit and doze while the old man would dance and chant to the rising moon.

Eventually, Owl moved into the medicine man's lodge, to be more readily available. The cooking of Crow Woman, he decided, was not up to the standards of his mother. However, she was a pleasant, kindly old woman, who now gave to Owl the affection she had never been able to bestow on a child of her own. Owl came to love the old couple as family. He still spent much of his infrequent spare time in the lodge of his parents, however.

When the grass began to green the following year, White Buffalo carefully instructed his assistant in the burning of the prairie. It was necessary, he pointed out, to watch, almost daily, the growth of certain of the grasses. When they became so tall, he indicated on a gnarled forefinger, it was time to burn. Too early, there would be no proper greening. Too late, it would burn poorly and destroy much new growth. Then the buffalo would not come.

Owl was impressed by the awesome responsibility for the decision. He had always regarded the annual event as something that just happened.

Apparently the decision was right, for the prairie did green, and the buffalo did come.

Now, announced White Buffalo, it was time for Owl to learn to work within the herd. First there was an impressive dance ceremony in the lodge. The old man put on the white buffalo headdress of his office and began his dance, while Crow Woman beat a rhythm on a small drum.

The white headdress, with horns attached and the skin of the hump falling down around the old man's shoulders, was very strong medicine. It had been among the People for many generations, Owl knew, handed down with the name from one medicine man to the next. The young man could still hardly comprehend that some day he might be the one to wear that scared cape.

Owl tried to watch carefully as the medicine man performed the dance. He sat in awe as the old man leaned stiffly over, the massive head swaying in mimicry of the buffalo's movements. The feet pawed at the floor in perfect imitation of a buffalo bull with the herd. This rendition, Owl realized, had taken a lifetime to learn.

At the end of the dance, White Buffalo took a tanned calfskin and spread it around the head and shoulders of his student. In this way, he stated, would the boy begin to learn.

They began by approaching an undisturbed herd of buffalo. From the hilltop, White Buffalo pointed out things about the herd . . . the old cow who was probably the leader, standing on the far side . . . the largest old bull, but probably not the most dangerous . . . a young cow with a small calf, unpredictable and quite likely to attack if provoked.

"You must learn how the buffalo feels," the old man advised. "You must look at an animal and put yourself inside his head. How would you move if you were that calf, there?" He pointed with a crooked finger at a yellow calf, playfully trotting near its mother.

For days, Owl was permitted only to watch the animals. Then, with the calfskin over his shoulders, he mimicked the gaits of the live animals, under his teacher's inspection. The medicine man was noncommittal.

"Not good, not bad," he shrugged.

Next day, however, he suggested that Owl begin approaching the herd.

"If an animal threatens you," he advised, "remember how the calf does. He moves just enough, not too far. To run would give away your secret."

At first it was the hardest thing Owl had ever done. With the calfskin over his shoulder, he moved among the big animals, pretending to be one of them, although a small one. Owl was sure he would be discovered, and at very least send the herd flying over the hill. At worst, he imagined himself trampled or gored.

Owl realized finally that he must be doing it right. He had not frightened the herd, and had not been trampled or gored. The incident which really convinced him was an accident. While watching a possibly dangerous young cow, he backed accidentally into the flank of a large bull. The massive head swung irritably, a polished black horn brushed his shoulder, and Owl jumped quickly aside. Just as a calf would jump, he realized later. Maybe, he thought that night, I really am getting inside the head of the buffalo.

However, Owl was beginning to resent this constant preoccupation with buffalo. He could see that when the old man had learned his profession, this had been an important part. It had been necessary to work among the buffalo, to learn how to move the herd without alarming the animals. They could be maneuvered into a narrow confine or stampeded over a cliff to assist the hunters. White Buffalo had told him endless tales of such hunts.

But now, with the hunting done on horseback, what was the use? The hunt was fast, open, and moving rapidly. There was no place for a medicine man on foot among the animals.

Owl ventured to raise this question one evening. White Buffalo became irritated.

"You will learn these things because I say so," he snapped. "All things begin at the beginning. And you have a long way before you begin to be a medicine man!"

Owl still had his doubts, but was wise enough to keep them to himself.

3

It **was in** his sixteenth summer that Owl was pro-
nounced qualified to assume the duties of his office.
White Buffalo had allowed Owl to make the decision on
the spring burning time this season, although he himself
had made the announcement. Now, he advised his young
assistant, there remained only one thing. His vision.

The old man explained in some detail the procedure
required, although Owl knew it well. White Buffalo was
becoming more forgetful, and repeated himself often.

"You must go out into the hills alone. You must eat nothing and talk to no one for three days, or until your vision
comes. It may be in a dream or awake, that your medicine
animal comes to you. You must tell no one his name when
you return to the People."

Owl nodded. He embraced Crow Woman, picked up
his weapons and his robe, and stepped out into the sunlight of a crisp day in the Ripening Moon. He stopped

briefly at his parents' lodge and then strode rapidly up the slope and out of sight.

He knew exactly where he was going. A day's journey to the southwest was a high, flat-topped mesa. Owl had been there before. From its crest one could see in all directions to the edge of the world. What better place, he thought, to fast and wait for one's vision? He filled a water skin at a spring, and climbed the hill just as Sun Boy carried his torch below the western rim.

Owl spread his robe and lay down, watching the stars come out. He wondered what to do next, and felt a little foolish. It had been many moons since he had had absolutely nothing to do. Then he felt guilty for having almost felt that his vision seeking was a waste of time. He mentally apologized to his yet-unknown medicine animal as he drifted off to sleep.

Owl awoke with the sun in his face and the prairie alive with the morning. He was hungry. He wondered if it were permissible to admit to hunger, and decided that it was. He passed the day watching the distant herds of buffalo and antelope, and singing to himself some of the chants of the medicine man. He drank a little from his water skin, and slept. The following day was a repeat of the last.

When he returned to the village, he would be recognized as a medicine man. He wondered idly when he would assume the title "White Buffalo." Immediately, or at some future time? The name must be given away by the old man before his death. It would be up to him, when and how it would be accomplished, Owl supposed. He was still hungry as he drifted to sleep again.

The next day the hunger was gone. He felt exhilarated, light-headed, yet strong. He felt that he could see things clearly, no matter how far. He could almost step off the mesa and fly, like the buzzards circling below him. This alarming thought brought him back to reality, and he spent the day in thought, sometimes sleeping for a short while. That night came the dreams.

It began as he dozed off, with the sound of a distant coyote's chuckling song in his ears. The young man drifted in and out of consciousness. Part of the time the chortling cry was that of an actual animal beyond the hill. Then it became a segment of a confused dream, in which his grandfather, the Coyote, chuckled at his confusion. In one of his half-awake moments, Owl realized that this was the reason for his grandfather's name. His chuckling giggle sounded exactly like the call of the animal on the hill. He smiled and drifted deeper.

In his dreams, various animals came past the spot where he sat. Some spoke to him, others only looked curiously. But he found that either way, he could see "inside the head" as he had learned to do with the buffalo. He felt the constant anxiety of the rabbit, and the searching of the red-tailed hawk as he circled the meadow. The deer, cautious and ready to retreat, looked at him a long moment.

"You are one of us," came the thought of a gigantic buffalo bull as he grazed past without looking up.

A coyote came and sat next to him, chuckling quietly. Then suddenly it was his grandfather, who reminded him again, "White Buffalo would not take you as his helper, unless he saw your strength and wisdom. But it will be hard—"

The coyote, now an animal again, rose and trotted out of sight. This, thought Owl, though he was still dreaming, must be my medicine animal. He drifted to sleep again.

He was roused this time by a group of bears who ambled into his dreams. They stood over him, talking in their own language. He was puzzled for a moment. Why had he seen so easily inside the heads of all the other animals, but could not understand the language of these bears?

One of the bears stepped close and rose on its hind legs, outlined against the rising sun. The other bears stepped close, also, and rose to full height. Alarmed, Owl opened his eyes to escape this disagreeable vision.

The sun was rising. The bears were still there, not in a dream. But they were not bears now, either. They were men. Owl had never seen any of them before, but he could tell by their garments and weapons that they were not of the People. They were the enemy, the dreaded Head Splitters.

Reflex flung the young man into action. His weapons were out of reach, but his hand closed on a fist-sized rock and flung it at the face of the closest warrior. The man fell backward, blood streaming from his broken nose. Owl flung himself with a rush on another man, and was accrediting himself quite well when he was grasped from behind by several pairs of hands. His captors threw him roughly to the ground and tied hands and feet behind him.

The man with the broken nose approached, furious, with a heavy club to end the matter, but was restrained by the others. There was laughter at his appearance, blood smeared over face and hands.

A man who was apparently the leader of the party stepped forward to question the prisoner. Owl understood not one word of the language used, but the other accompanied his questions with the hand gestures of the universal sign language.

"How are you called? What are you doing here?"

The ludicrous situation struck Owl, even under the circumstances. They could not understand his spoken answer, and he could not use sign language with his hands tied. He motioned with his head toward his bound hands. The young chief who was the leader stepped forward to cut the thongs, brushing aside the protests of Broken Nose.

"You have no right to treat me in this way," signed Owl. "I am the son of a chief!"

General laughter followed. Then one of the men stepped forward with a sudden exclamation. He pulled sharply at the fringe of new hair along Owl's upper lip, and murmured excitedly. The others murmured too. The leader motioned them to silence, and rapidly signed a new question.

"Your father is the Hairface, chief of the Elk-dog band of the People?"

Owl did not answer, but it was too late. He knew he had made a grave mistake in revealing his identity. His captors were talking among themselves, pleased and excited. *Aiee,* not every day does one capture the son of an enemy chief!

4

For the first few days, Owl fought the idea of captivity constantly. The first night, he spent most of the time of darkness chewing at his bonds. The rawhide thongs became slippery and elastic in his mouth, and he was actually beginning to feel some loosening in the tension on his wrists. Then, when the sky was beginning to pale with the false dawn, his efforts were discovered by the sentry.

The man cuffed the fettered Owl around the head and ears, and calmly retied his hands. Behind his back, this time. From the confident way that the guard laughed and joked about the incident, Owl believed that he had been perfectly aware of the prisoner's efforts for most of the night. The young man sank into depression.

He would spend the uncomfortable time of darkness, hands tied tightly behind him, in wakeful unrest. After three nights, he began to recover from his gloom and spend the time in more productive thought. His training under the old medicine man began to manifest itself.

"You look, but you do not see," White Buffalo had once scolded in his early training. "You must look behind the things that show, for the meaning beyond."

In another culture and time, it might have been called analytic observation. To Owl, the process was only that of summing up all the available information and then acting on it. Never too hastily, the old man had constantly warned him. Gain all possible facts first. In the stress of the present situation, Owl had reverted to emotional reaction. Now, with time to reason and think, he became the shrewd, trained observer that White Buffalo had attempted to create.

Then, too, there was the visit from his medicine animal. Owl had just slipped into a fitful slumber one night. His hands were uncomfortably tied behind him as he lay, partially on his side. In his half-sleep, the young man heard the distant call of a coyote, and the answer of the animal's mate. Then, in the strange dream-state, a coyote came and sat beside him as before. This time, nothing was said, but he felt a warm confidence and a change in his entire attitude. It was somehow reassuring that his medicine animal could still visit him and possibly help him, even in captivity. Next morning Owl was almost cheerful.

His more cooperative attitude began to be productive immediately. He received more and better food, and his bonds were not drawn so uncomfortably tight. He was able to pay more attention to such things as direction of travel. He found that the war party was moving in a generally southwest direction. This he observed by the path of Sun Boy during the day. By night, this observation was verified by the position of the Seven Hunters and their relation to the constant real-star in the north.

He would need to know which way led back to his own people after his escape. Owl had no doubts as to whether he could escape. Only when. In his mind, escape was inevitable, unless he were killed first. And it seemed reasonable to assume that if he appeared cooperative, they would be less likely to kill him.

True, one of the warriors seemed determined to accomplish that end. The man Owl now thought of as Broken Nose constantly harassed the captive. He would sit directly in front of the young man, fondling his knife and making suggestive gestures. He would slowly draw the blade across the front of his own throat. His motions clearly suggested what he intended ultimately for the prisoner. On other occasions Broken Nose would use the universal hand sign language, accompanied by obscene gestures. His leer would rove to the area of Owl's genitals, as he suggestively handled the knife.

Perhaps most nerve-wracking of all was the game the man played with a war club. He would creep quietly behind where Owl lay. Then suddenly, with a shout, he would smash the club's heavy stone to the ground just a finger's breadth from portions of the prisoner's anatomy.

Owl soon observed that the leader of the war party was considerably annoyed by these antics. Several times he spoke curtly to Broken Nose. The young man began to regard this man as his protector. In any case, he was sure that without the restraining influence he would have long since been killed or mutilated or both. And, he was afraid, not necessarily in that order. His skin crawled with terror at the obscene threats of Broken Nose, though he attempted to conceal it. He would show them that a chief's son could greet death with dignity.

This bold face-down with death proved not immediately necessary, however. After a few days' travel the war party reached an encampment of lodges, apparently of their own band. Various of the men were greeted by women and children. Much ado was made of the prisoner. Owl was jeered and pelted with rocks and sticks by the children. Dogs barked and nipped at his feet as he plodded at the end of a rope behind his captor's horse. An old woman hobbled alongside, jabbering toothlessly, and spat into his face.

All this did not bother Owl, particularly. He had expected it. He had seen prisoners of his own people treated similarly. This was merely the initial expression of contempt for an enemy captive.

More worrisome was the thought stirring uneasily in the back of his mind. What would be his ultimate fate? Public torture was a strong possibility. Owl had little knowledge of the niceties of Head Splitter torture. None of the People did. For good reason, too, he thought grimly. He knew of no one who had survived torture by this dreaded enemy. Thoughts of escape faded.

A horrible thing flitted across his mind. It was known that some tribes, far to the south, ate human flesh. Owl could not recall ever having heard that of the Head Splitters. Of course not, he reassured himself, with more confidence than he actually felt. The Head Splitters might hold him to sell or trade back to his own people. He would be more valuable to them for that purpose than for food. Still, the thought sent chills up his spine as he plodded through the thick dust of the enemy village.

His captor halted the horse before one of the largest of the lodges, and slid to the ground. An assortment of women and children welcomed the man warmly. Strange, thought Owl. He had never considered the fact that the enemy, the dreaded killers, must have a family life, too. This scene, except for the different ornamentation and slightly varying construction of the skin lodges, could have been in his own village.

The returned warrior took the rope from Owl's neck, and retied the young man's hands behind him, as had become the custom for the night. The man handed the other end of the rope to an old woman standing near the lodge doorway. There was general laughter, then a few more words of explanation from his captor. More laughter, exclamations of awe, and some jeers from the older children.

Owl began to realize the situation. This man, probably a chief, claimed Owl as his prisoner. It would be a matter of great prestige to hold the son of an enemy chief as a captive. And, to further the humiliation, he was being turned over to the women. This in itself was a threatening circumstance. Among Owl's own people, it was regarded that the women of the tribe could be relied on to create new refinements of cruelty in torture. True, this was not the case in Owl's immediate family. His parents, in fact, rather disapproved of excessive torture of prisoners. But some individuals among the People were noted for their imaginative deeds in this area. Owl shuddered a little, and hoped that the family of his captor was not so inclined. And, there was the ever present threat of Broken Nose and his avowed intentions.

The old woman shuffled over, examined Owl like a warrior sizing up a new horse, and then jerked on his rope. He moved in the indicated direction, and she motioned him to sit. The rope was then tied, with only a few handspans' slack, to the base of a lodge pole. Any attempt to escape, he realized, would rattle the lodge cover and warn the occupants.

The young man tried to maintain a dignified and confident manner. It was a difficult task, he discovered, while sitting in the dirt among yapping dogs, and with hands tied behind him. His captor's family trooped into the lodge. Much later, one of the younger women returned, and half threw him a bone with shreds of meat.

Then, as an afterthought, she turned and retied his hands loosely in front of him. Now he could pick up the bone, and fend off the dogs while he ate. Owl signed his thanks, but the woman only nodded as she slipped back inside.

5

Owl soon found that things were much better for him if he cooperated. If he obeyed his captors, his treatment was tolerable, and he received food that was edible at fairly regular intervals. If not, he received many a whack with sticks from the women. In addition, he literally had to fight the dogs for such bones and offal as were thrown into the dust for him to eat.

Likewise, cheerful cooperation resulted in more freedom. His bonds were all but forgotten after a few days. He was tied only at night, and then later, when he showed no tendency to escape, not at all.

The young man was assigned work, of course. Hard, exhausting work. Carrying wood and water, preparing meat and skins for use. Women's work, in short. It was probably well that Owl did not fully understand this. The work assigned to him, that of women, was intended to be demeaning. It was some time before he grasped the subtle difference in attitude toward women among the Head Splitters. Among his own people, women were held in high regard. Some were heard in council, they could hold property, and basically were well respected. The Head Splitters, while demonstrating a certain love and affection for the women of the family, still seemed to regard them as possessions.

Just as he was regarded as a possession, he grimly decided after one exhausting day at the drudgery of butchering buffalo. He sill had no inkling as to his ultimate fate. Nothing of a very threatening nature seemed imminent, however.

Owl realized that the better he understood his captors, the better his chances for escape. Therefore, he set his powers of observation to work, learning all he could of the language and customs of the tribe. He found that he grasped the language without too much difficulty. Rather more rapidly than he expected, in fact. Owl was reaping the benefits of his strictly regimented training under the medicine man, old White Buffalo. How far away that part of his life seemed already.

Soon he could understand the major thrust of any conversation he happened to overhear. Granted, he could not have phrased an answering sentence. There were still many words completely foreign to his ears. Yet he could gain much information in this way. He elected to appear as ignorant as possible. This was greatly to his advantage in adding to his store of knowledge. His captors, believing him to be totally without understanding, would carry on conversations in his presence as if he were non-existent.

He began to gain knowledge not only of the language and customs of this Head Splitter band, but of the nebulous political structure. As in his own tribe, the shifting weight of prestige governed the actions of many of the people. His captor, he discovered, was called "Bull's Tail," and was one of the more respected of the sub-chiefs in the band.

Everyone seemed to think well of the man. His courage and integrity were above reproach. Bull's Tail had four wives, Owl observed, and several children. The taking of more than one wife, while not unusual among the People, was apparently much more common among the Head Splitters.

In fact, it became almost an obsession with some men, it seemed. One of the party which had originally captured Owl, the man Owl thought of as Broken Nose, was one of these. He had at least seven or eight wives, all very young, and some quite attractive. Owl was not surprised to learn that the man was called "Many Wives." His penchant for buying any young and attractive prisoner was well known in the tribe. It was regarded as something of a joke.

Owl found the practice repulsive, and quite foreign to the customs of his own people. He was already wary of the man, who still used every occasion to communicate his intentions of bodily harm to the prisoner. The man's preoccupation with possession of young women fanned the flames of enmity in Owl. Many Wives was apparently considered wealthy, and his ability to pay well for girls he found desirable was well known.

On one occasion, some days after Owl's captivity began, three men from another Head Splitter band arrived with a prisoner, a young woman. They had come, it appeared, solely for the purpose of selling the girl to the affluent Many Wives. Owl watched from a distance as haggling over the price took place before Many Wives' lodge. Apparently an exchange was agreed on, and the visitors departed, leading several horses.

This incident disturbed Owl immensely. The girl was very pretty. Although obviously unhappy, she carried herself proudly, and demonstrated spirit and courage that Owl found admirable. He realized that she, like himself, was a prisoner with little hope of escape. He became depressed for several days, at times almost despairing the possibility of any change in his miserable status.

The new girl was treated badly by Many Wives. That was apparent, even when observed from a distance. She was assigned the most distasteful tasks. Still, she maintained a proud demeanor. She kept her appearance neat and well-groomed, and even the way she walked and stood showed pride, Owl thought.

He benefited tremendously from observing this captive girl over the next few days. Her spirit was contagious, and he began to take more care of his own appearance. A captive slave-wife of a Head Splitter sub-chief could show proud example. Should not he, Owl, deport himself in a manner befitting the son of a chief of the People? His pride ultimately triumphed over his depression, and he regained a determination. Some day, no matter how long, he would escape and return to his position in his father's band, the Elk-dogs of the People.

It became apparent that any such plans must be indefinitely postponed, however. The Head Splitters began to make preparations to break camp. Owl gathered that they were to travel south to more comfortable wintering quarters. And away from his own people, he realized glumly. He must wait until the following season to make his escape attempt.

Still, it was probably well that the seasonal move was to take place. There had been frost in the air, as Cold Maker blew his chilling breath from the north. Owl had begun to snuggle at night among the dogs for warmth, outside the lodge of Bull's Tail. He had started to wonder how he was to survive a winter with no shelter except the scrap of ragged buffalo robe he had managed to possess.

For as many days as he had fingers and toes the band traveled, into strange, forbidding country. The Head Splitters seemed quite at home here, but to Owl it was the end of the earth. Sand, dust, spiny plants with strange growth habits. The grass, such as it was, seemed thin and poor when compared with the lush grasses of his prairie homeland.

The band had paused for a rest stop. Owl slid the heavy rawhide packs from his back and sank to a reclining position. He checked the ground carefully first, of course. He had never seen an area with so many small creatures that could bite or sting or inflict harm. And real-snakes! Only three suns past, a horse had died, horribly swollen and distorted, from the bite of the biggest real-snake Owl had ever seen. The snake had not, it was said, even bothered to rattle a warning.

After making sure of his reclining place, Owl relaxed his aching muscles and closed his eyes. He hoped the stop would be a long one. The load he had been forced to carry was a heavy and clumsy one. The exhausted young man was very near sleep when a soft voice broke through his consciousness. It was lilting and jaunty, almost mocking, yet sincere.

"Do not move, only listen," came the melodious feminine tones. "You wish to escape, man of the People?"

With a shock, Owl realized the woman was speaking in his own language, the tongue of the People, which he had not heard for several moons.

Owl sighed deeply, and flung an arm over his head, rolling over, as if shifting to a more comfortable position. Now on his side, he cautiously opened his eyes, only a slit at first. There, seated on a red sandstone boulder a few feet away, was a young woman. The slave girl, he realized, of Many Wives.

"Who are you?" He spoke cautiously and softly. "You are of the People?"

"I am called Willow. Mine is the Mountain band." She paused. "I saw you at the Big Council a summer ago. Your father is Heads Off, chief of the Elk-dog band." It was more a statement than a question. "I was taken by the Head Splitters in the Ripening Moon last season."

Voices approaching threatened to cut short the conversation. Owl muttered as if in sleep, and rolled to his back again.

"Are there others of the People here?"

"I know of only one old woman. Her spirit is broken and she will not wish to leave. But we must escape. We will talk again."

The girl's voice trailed off into a musical hum, and as the others approached, she seemed only to be softly singing to herself. Nearby lay the sleeping Owl.

Actual sleep did not come easily to Owl that night. His mind was filled to overflowing with thoughts of the girl and of escape. They must bide their time carefully, to avoid suspicion and wait for the proper moment. But his main feeling was that of happiness. What tremendous good fortune, to discover a woman of the People. One who appeared highly intelligent, capable, and best of all, one who was the most beautiful woman he had ever seen. How appropriate her name, Willow, to describe the way she walked and moved.

On a far hilltop a coyote called to her mate, and Owl, hearing, was almost exultant. His medicine animal was still with him. Good things were sure to result from the day's events.

6

The girl **was** tall, as were many of the women of the People. Owl's own mother was called the Tall One. This young woman, while not quite possessing the height of Tall One, was nearly as tall as Owl. She appeared to be about his own age. Her legs were gracefully shaped, and the supple resiliency of her long body gave promise of easy birthing.

Owl could not remember ever seeing a woman whom he found so physically attractive. Her large eyes reminded him of the gentle eyes of a deer. These reflected sadness and hard times, but there was a flash of spirit. The look of eagles, White Buffalo would have called it. In addition, the eyes could reflect a sparkle of joy and humor over the smallest thing. And, Owl reflected glumly, she had very few things, even small things, to cause her to show sparkle.

She continued to be an inspiration to him. Her appearance was always as carefully managed as if she were among her own people, taking a prominent place in the affairs of her tribe.

Her hair, he now noticed, was plaited in the style of the People. This she seemed to do as a defiant challenge to her captor, realizing that it might irritate the man. At any rate, it was a public proclamation that she was proud of her heritage. Prisoner though she might be, at least for the moment, she was, above all, a woman of the People.

The young people found occasion to be near each other whenever they could. Owl would try to casually encounter the girl while out gathering dung or firewood, or in the event of a buffalo kill, to work in close proximity to her. Willow cooperated in these efforts, but frequently warned him to be careful. They must not arouse suspicion. They intently practiced looking glum and dejected. It was extremely difficult to appear morose, however, when an occasion offered for them to be together.

This became one of the strangest of all courtships. Both parties in servitude, and Willow ostensibly the wife of another man. They could hardly look or smile at each other, which became very frustrating Touching, of course, was next to impossible.

They did manage, once, to clasp hands for the space of a few heartbeats. Bull's Tail and Many Wives had shared a kill, a fat buffalo cow. Several of the women of both lodges were busily butchering out the animal, each trying to maintain claim to the choicest cuts and most desirable organs.

Soon the two captives found themselves working side by side, up to the elbows in entrails in the body cavity. Owl grasped the girl's hand, deeply out of sight, and she returned the quick squeeze.

The jealous Many Wives, however, riding past at the moment, struck Willow across the back with his quirt. He scolded her for malingering, then sent her back to the lodge with a load of meat. He turned to Owl in a quiet rage.

"And you, son of a snake, will be killed very slowly if you do not stay away from my wives!"

Owl dropped his eyes submissively and continued his work. It had been a foolhardy thing to do, and now they had aroused suspicion. They would now have to be more cautious than ever. He silently cursed himself for a fool, at the same time smarting under the blow that the girl had received.

If the truth were known, Many Wives had seen nothing at all. Only his resentment against anyone who appeared happy at his work had brought forth the surly reaction. Nevertheless, the incident further fanned the smoldering enmity between the two. Many Wives would cheerfully have killed or maimed the prisoner at any opportunity.

Owl, for his part, could hardly stand the thoughts of the ugly, sadistic Head Splitter taking Willow to his sleeping robes as a wife. He could think of innumerable variations of torture for the man. Owl realized that this was inconsistent with his general attitude toward the practice of torture, but this was a special case. Many Wives, he felt, had forfeited any right to consideration. He devoutly hoped that when the time came for their escape, he would somehow be able to kill the surly Many Wives. This became almost an obsession with Owl during the course of the winter. Only in this way, he felt, could he avenge the mistreatment of the captive girl. Owl had already begun to think of Willow as his own.

The Head Splitters established winter quarters, and life became a little easier for Owl. There was not quite so much menial work, since hunting had slowed considerably. He was still expected to carry firewood and water.

On very cold nights Owl was permitted to crouch just inside the skin doorway of the lodge. Grudgingly, of course. The first time he tried it he was whacked and berated, and was expecting to be turned back out into the sleeting rain. Just as he began to despair the possibility of surviving without shelter, Bull's Tail intervened.

"Let him stay," he ordered casually, without looking up from the bone he was gnawing.

Owl was careful not to tempt his good fortune too far. On any night when it was at all possible, he was outside with the dogs. Without thinking the matter out completely, he still had escape in the back of his mind. That escape would be easier if he were not encumbered with such things as tie thongs on the lodge doorway in case of a hasty exit.

One shocking incident occurred during the Moon of Long Nights. A group of young men, hunting in the area near the winter camp, had discovered a cave. In the course of the exploration, they had roused a hibernating she-bear and her two cubs. In the melee, one of the hunters had been horribly mauled, and they had killed the bear and one cub. The other cub had escaped.

The hunting party returned in triumph, and to Owl's horror, a feast of bear meat was planned. Among the People, the bear was a forbidden animal. After all, did not bears walk upright like a man? To kill a bear, except in self-defense, was very bad medicine. To actually eat the flesh was, in the mind of the young man, the equivalent of cannibalism.

Equally revolting was the spectacle of one of the hunters, he who claimed the kill. The man walked around the camp, flauntingly wearing the skin of the cub around his shoulders as a cape.

Owl was completely repulsed by this defiance of decency. Nothing in his captivity had he found so distasteful, except, of course, the abuse of the girl.

He watched from a distance the celebration and the dance reenacting the kill. He was sick, spiritually and physically. His strict training in the ways of the medicine man made the situation even worse for him. The deliberate infraction of a medicine taboo was beyond his understanding.

Willow, watching the dejected Owl, was sympathetic, but not touched so deeply. She observed the custom of the People by refusing participation in the feast. However, she was able to be more objective about the situation. Medicine taboos, she realized, were different for different tribes—for different individuals, even. She remembered a man of her own tribe whose taboo had been antelope. From some vision or vow of long ago, he avoided the flesh of the animal entirely. He had been called "Eats-no-Antelope" behind his back by the children, she recalled whimsically. At any rate, Willow decided, the medicine taboo of others is their own concern. She could be much more tolerant than the strictly disciplined Owl.

Despite such cultural clashes, the seasons moved on. The Moon of Snows was considerably milder than the People were accustomed to further to the north. There were only a few days when the snow lay on the earth. Likewise, the Moon of Hunger brought no major hardships. A few families fell back on the eating of dogs, the ever-present provision. Basically, however, enough meat and pemmican had been prepared and stored to supply the winter. Those who ate dogs did so by choice, or to enjoy a meal of fresh meat for variation in the diet.

When the warm south breezes of the Wakening Moon began to bring the smell of moist earth, Owl became impatient. He thought that the decision to move north, back to more familiar territory, would never come. But at last, late in the Greening Moon, the Head Splitters began to prepare for the move.

Owl was elated. He already felt that he was starting home. The details of planning an escape were secondary, compared to the fact that they were now headed for familiar territory. He wondered if White Buffalo had fired the grass yet. It was hard to tell. The plants in this arid region were so different. The young medicine man needed the familiar grasses of the prairie to make his estimate.

After the travelers reached the grasslands, there was one frustrating incident. The band was spread in a straggling column across the prairie when suddenly an excited murmur rippled down the line. Owl caught the word which he had learned the Head Splitters used for the People. His father's own band, perhaps? If there were fighting, there was the possibility of escape. He looked around for Willow, but did not see her.

The band moved quickly into a compact group, children in the center, then the women, with warriors around the outside. Owl, with a few others who were captives of a sort, and potential troublemakers, were herded near the center of the circle. He felt a sharp prick on the side of his neck and glanced around. The old woman, the mother of Bull's Tail, he now knew, showed him the point of her skinning knife.

"You will be silent," she signed. "If there is fighting, you are the first to die!"

"Of course, Mother," answered Owl, also in the sign language.

He knew fighting was unlikely. Both groups would have their women and children; and would avoid conflict. He had seen such chance meetings almost annually, and had watched, fascinated, from the center of the circle. Now he did so again, peering around and between the horses carrying baggage or pulling pole-drags.

A column of travelers began to file over the hill, heading in a generally northerly direction, but at a slightly different tangent from that of the Head Splitters. Three men moved their horses out from the Head Splitters' band, and riders from the approaching group slowly moved out to meet them.

Owl recognized old White Bear, chief of the People's Red Rocks band. The Red Rocks had frequent contact with the Head Splitters because of geographic location. The chiefs of the rival tribes pulled their horses to a stop and sat calmly in discussion. Owl could see the sign language fairly well. They would, he knew, comment on the weather, the availability of game, and the general condition of the grassland. There would be a few derogatory taunts by both sides, but no open conflict. He wondered if the Head Splitters would use the obvious taunt: the capture of the son of a chief of the People. He could see no such sign, and decided that he had not been mentioned. After all, this was not his father's band.

The two enemy columns cautiously circled and parted. Owl watched the People file over the hill with a deep longing. If only he and Willow could escape within the next few suns, they should have little trouble finding protection with the Red Rocks. Even though neither of them belonged to this most southwestern band of the People, they were, after all, the People. Owl had many acquaintants in the Red Rocks band. He knew that they would be welcome in the lodge of White Bear, who was his father's friend of long standing.

Yes, he mused, as the column started off again and he shouldered his packs. The time for escape must be soon.

7

Despite the feeling of urgency, the escape opportunity did not present itself immediately. The captives were closely watched. Owl finally realized that the possibility of protection by the Red Rocks band would be as obvious to their captors as to himself. He irritably resumed the routine chores required of him.

The Head Splitters established a summer encampment, and the easy-living activities of the Growing Moon and the Moon of Roses moved along. Hunting was good, and the prisoners were kept busy with the associated drudgery.

It was not until the Moon of Thunder that the escape came. The night was warm and the air fragrant. Owl was tired, and had rolled into his robe outside the lodge of Bull's Tail without a thought of anything but rest.

Just past the setting of the partial moon, when the time of darkness was at its blackest, a soft voice whispered in his ear.

"Come quickly, man of the People! Here, carry this."

He took the bundle, tossed his robe over his shoulder, and sleepily stumbled after the graceful shape ahead of him in the night.

They threaded their way among the lodges, once pausing to threaten a restless dog. Soon they were on the open prairie, circling cautiously to avoid the guards at the horse herd. At last they stopped, breathless, and Willow swept into his arms in a warm embrace. Owl would have prolonged the moment, but she gently disengaged herself.

"Come," she murmured, "we will stop later."

They moved rapidly in a northerly direction, guiding on the real-star. For the first time, they were able to converse freely, a luxury beyond belief. They chattered happily as they traveled.

She had, Willow told him, been secretly building a supply of food to be used in the escape. That was the bundle Owl was now carrying. She had waited until the proper time, when Many Wives was exhausted from amorous activity, and the night was pleasant enough for Owl to be sleeping outside.

The constellation of the Seven Hunters had moved for some distance around the real-star when the girl stopped suddenly. They were in a small starlit meadow, the musical sound of a cold spring tinkling from the slope above. She moved to a level spot near the stream, and spread her robe on the soft grass.

"Here," she announced, "we will spend our first night together."

The young people were faced with a certain conflict. Both had grown up in the strict moral and ethical ways of the People, regarding marriage customs. Yet both realized the urgency of the situation. They must take whatever opportunity offered to cling together. By morning, they might both be dead.

They solved this minor dilemma simply and beautifully,

by enacting the ritual of the People. Taking the corners of Owl's ragged robe, they drew it around their shoulders, enveloping both in a single cloak, to signify the marriage bond.

Owl's amateurish ineptness was offset by his gentle and considerate nature. As for Willow, her experience, although more extensive, had been totally without affection. Never was a marriage contract consummated with more sincerity and devotion.

Some time later, in the dark before the dawn, she whispered in his ear.

"Wake, my husband, we must travel."

Sluggishly and regretfully, the two prepared for departure. A last look around the little meadow where their life together had begun, and they started northward. They struck a good pace, chewing strips of the dried meat Willow had brought as provisions. By dawn they had greatly increased the distance from the enemy camp.

But not enough, Owl was afraid. Looking ahead, he could see several days' travel over the rolling plain. There was very little opportunity for hiding, as there would have been in more broken country among the rocky hillsides. Their captors were sure to follow, probably on horseback. They had made a major error in judgment in not stealing horses for the escape.

Owl was certain that the girl realized their situation too, but neither voiced doubts. They traveled as rapidly as was practical, trying to ignore the fact that behind them somewhere was a pursuing party of angry Head Splitters.

Owl first saw them from the top of a low ridge. There were six riders, intent on the trail of the refugees. They were closer than he had hoped, and would probably overtake the couple before Sun Boy's torch stood overhead.

He looked ahead over the plain. There could hardly have been a worse area for hiding. In many places, gullies and small canyons would have furnished at least some help, but here there was nothing. A small stream wandered across the flat, and he motioned in that direction.

Their pace necessarily slowed as they attempted to conceal the back trail by stepping on rocks in the stream bed. Owl, with a sinking feeling, realized that this ruse, the only one available, would be obvious to the pursuers.

Then, like a gift in time of need, he saw a possible hiding place. A few hundred paces away, in the open grassland, lay the rotting carcass of a buffalo. An old bull, by the size of it. Probably one of the aging outcasts that followed the herds, gradually becoming weaker with advancing infirmities until pulled down by wolves. The fugitives turned aside, attempting to leave as little sign of their passing as possible.

Hurriedly, they approached the remains. As Owl had hoped, the dry air of the high plains had preserved the skin somewhat. Coyotes and vultures had stripped a good portion of the meat from the skeleton, but the massive rib cage was intact. The drying skin was pulled tightly across the bones like a lodge cover, and the huge body cavity was empty, cleaned out by the carrion eaters. He peered inside, making certain there was no real-snake or other creature of harm. Then the two squeezed through.

The quarters were cramped and smelly, but secure. The more exposed portion of their little retreat was camouflaged somewhat by stuffing Owl's ragged robe up against the inside of the opening. The fur blended well with that of the dead carcass, or at least Owl hoped so.

He peered through a jagged hole in the skin, and soon saw the horsemen, intently following the trail in the stream bed. They had not been deceived in the least. He identified Many Wives, and a couple of his friends. Bull's Tail was also present, and this proved encouraging to Owl. At least, he might be able to furnish them some protection from the excesses of the hot-tempered Many Wives.

As the search party came to a point opposite their hiding

place, one rider reined his horse around and cantered easily over to examine the dead buffalo. The fugitives crouched, hardly daring to breathe, as he circled the carcass. Finally, he thrust a spear into the body cavity, as if to satisfy his curiosity, and then, with scarcely a backward glance, turned and loped away.

Owl had felt the girl flinch against him when the spear thrust came. He looked questioningly, but she smiled at him.

"It is nothing, my husband."

He saw a narrow trickle of blood down the shapely calf.

"It is only a scratch," she reassured again.

The search party had now drawn away and were nearly beyond the shoulder of the next hill. Owl was pondering their next move. The cramped, odorous quarters were becoming unpleasant.

As soon as the Head Splitters were out of sight, they crawled from the hiding place and moved to the thin shelter of the willows along the stream. The girl limped only a little.

No sooner had they reached the dubious concealment, however, than voices were heard again. The warriors were returning. The man who had investigated the dead buffalo was leading the way, gesturing and pointing. They headed straight for the carcass. Owl caught the words "blood" and "spear," and realized the unfortunate quirk of fate. The man had noticed fresh blood on the point of his spear, and realized that a dead and dried buffalo carcass does not bleed.

They circled the carcass, and one man, apparently a skilled tracker, discovered a drop of blood on the grass. He straightened, glanced around, and then pointed directly at their hiding place.

In a moment the two were surrounded, seized roughly, and thrown to the ground. Many Wives, livid with rage, stood over the helpless Owl, as others tied his hands.

"I will stop this offspring of a dog from stealing men's wives," he shouted.

He grasped the thong holding Owl's breechclout and quickly severed it with his knife. His hand grasped at the young man as Owl struggled helplessly.

A blood-curdling scream from Willow caught the attention of Many Wives. He straightened to see the girl twist free from her captors and spring across the prairie. Two men leaped back on their horses in pursuit as the others watched, laughing.

In horror, Owl saw the horsemen approach the running girl. He realized that she had attempted to save him by drawing attention to herself. She dodged between the horses and they wheeled to catch her. One man swung his club and the girl was tossed into the grass like a broken doll. They turned and trotted back.

Owl did not care what happened now. He felt that his life had just ended. An argument developed between Many Wives, who insisted on revenge, and Bull's Tail, who claimed ownership of the prisoner. For a moment the two nearly came to blows, and then Many Wives petulantly struck out at the prisoner with the handle of his war club. It caught the helpless Owl along the temple, and merciful blackness descended.

8

When Owl regained consciousness, it was because of a continuous jarring motion which caused his head to throb. Even then, a thought flitted through his mind. He was thankful that it was his head and not his groin that throbbed. Cautiously, he attempted to reassure himself that his anatomy was intact, and found that he was bound, his hands in front of him.

He was riding on a pole-drag, and his companion was the old woman. Slowly, he realized that he had been brought back to the camp of the Head Splitters, and that the band was now on the move again. He wondered how long he had been unconscious. More than a sun, he thought. He was still quite confused and snatches of memory kept returning unexpectedly.

The memory of the beautiful Willow tormented him, and for a time he wished that he had been killed, too. The ecstasy they had shared had been all too brief. Gradually he began to realize that the girl would want him to keep his courage. She had never wavered. He would owe it to the memory of this courageous woman, his wife of one ecstatic night, to keep his spirit. He must try again to escape.

The direction of travel was southwest, bending gradually more westerly. The band marched as if a long journey was anticipated.

He was treated harshly, though he was given reasonable amounts of food. Never was there a time when he was not watched closely by at least one of the women. His hands and feet were constantly tied except for very brief periods. The wrists and ankles became chafed and raw. Owl stopped struggling to free his bonds for the simple reason that the attempt was too painful.

As his strength returned, he was sometimes allowed to walk, with hands still tied, alongside the old woman's pole-drag.

The journey continued. They were much further to the west than in the previous season. Further west, Owl believed, than any of the People had ever been. At least, none had ever returned to tell of it.

One day, with Sun Boy's torch directly overhead, a murmur of excitement flickered down from the front of the column. Apparently they were nearing a destination of some sort.

Owl raised his head and peered forward, to see a village ahead. It consisted of lodges that were permanent in appearance, like the pole and mud lodges of the Growers. The People often visited tribes of Growers along the larger streams of the plains. Skins, furs, and meat had been traded for products of the farming tribes for many generations.

This permanent-appearing town, however, consisted of lodges of a type Owl had never seen before. They were taller than those of the Growers, flat on the tops instead of arched, and were squarish rather than round. Strangest of all, there seemed to be no door-skins. In fact, Owl could see no way at all to enter these lodges. Door-skins on lodges of the People always faced southeast. Owl thought at first perhaps all the doorways were on the other side.

As they passed among the strange dwellings, however, it became apparent that there were no openings on any side. He finally realized, after seeing some small children standing on top of the lodges, that this must be the mode of entry. His observation was verified by noting a young man climbing up the outside of a lodge on a device made of poles tied together.

The visiting Head Splitters stopped just outside the far perimeter of the village, and prepared to make camp. Several of the chiefs walked back into the jumble of mud lodges. Owl supposed they would pay their respects to the chief of the Mud Lodge people.

As darkness gathered, he watched the people of the strange tribe move among the lodges. The weather was mild, and much of the cooking seemed to be done outside. He was especially startled to see a woman busily tending a fire in a small conical lodge of mud, no taller than her head. Eventually she reached in with a long stick and brought out large lumps of some hot substance which must be food. The strange smell was pleasant to his nostrils.

Owl wondered if the People would believe his tales when he returned home. A tribe which built square lodges and climbed in and out through the smoke-hole on poles tied together! The cooking of strange foods in a special fire-lodge. His chances of being able to tell of these wondrous things looked pretty slim at the moment.

Full darkness had now fallen, and the people of his captors' tribe drew nearer their fires against the night's chill. Owl could see some of the Mud Lodge people climbing to the tops of their lodges to disappear inside. The delegation from the Head Splitters' camp returned, the men going separate ways to their own families.

Bull's Tail strode over, beckoned to Owl, and drew him

aside. He began to speak in the Head Splitter tongue, augmented by the sign language.

"I have exchanged you to this tribe. You have been nothing but trouble since you were captured. Many Wives will kill you if he is able." He paused and gave a long sigh. "I had hoped to keep you, for the honor of holding a chief's son, but—" he spread his hands in a shrug.

Owl was startled at the lengthy speech by his captor, and by his use of the Head Splitters' tongue. He must have known all along that his prisoner was gaining knowledge of the language.

Bull's Tail tied the hands of the captive in front of him, and led him among the mud lodges. Slowly, the enormity of this turn of events sank into Owl's mind. He was resentful and indignant, and felt betrayed by a man he had respected. Owl wondered wryly if Bull's Tail considered that he had brought a good price.

They reached a spot beside one of the dwellings, where two men of the Mud Lodge people waited, and they motioned him to climb. One of the men followed him up to the top of the structure, where another waited. Here they motioned to a smoke-stained hole and pushed him in that direction. Owl, remembering that cooperation had earned better treatment, moved over and started to climb down the ladder. One of the men stopped him long enough to untie his hands, and again motioned to the interior.

Owl descended into the warm, foul-smelling structure, coughing a little from the smoke. A small fire burned in the center of the lodge, and he could see the dark shapes of several men and boys around the edge of the darkness. Someone above pulled the ladder up and out of the smoke-hole. To Owl, accustomed to the wide skies and open horizons of the prairie, this was the most fearful of all sensations, that of entrapment. Never, in all the coming moons, did he entirely overcome this panicky feeling in one of these lodges when the pole-ladder was removed and the exit became inaccessible.

He glanced around the lodge, at the several faces reflecting light of the tiny fire. The thing he saw in each pair of eyes was disconcerting. Each was a replica of the last, revealing one thought. Hopelessness.

By the variety of the tattered garments that they wore, and the difference in the appearance of their hair, Owl judged that they represented several different tribes. He must attempt communication.

"Who are you?" he signed to the group at large. Only stares in answer. His inquiring glance touched each of the handful of faces in the lodge.

"Do you understand the signs?"

Surely, any tribe Owl had ever heard of could communicate with the universal hand signs. There was no change in the fixed expressions of despair.

"Are we all prisoners here?"

A man coughed, behind him in the corner. Owl turned to look. The tired old man chuckled without mirth, and began to sign.

"Of course we are prisoners, Stupid One!"

Owl did not answer, but sought an unoccupied place next to the wall and sat down. He wondered if it would be possible to create enough spirit in these men to attempt escape.

No matter, he thought. If they will not, at least I will.

9

Once a day a container of food was lowered, and the prisoners squabbled over the best positions around the vessel. There was little variety. Stewed corn or beans or a combination of the two. Sometimes only a mushy whitish substance which Owl identified as made of ground corn. How he longed for the rich, juicy flavor of hump ribs after a successful buffalo hunt. He would dream at night of feasting on good red meat until his belly hurt. Then he would awake, his belly actually hurting, but from hunger pangs. He wondered how long a person could live without meat, the staple of the People's diet.

Perhaps even worse was the inactivity. The most stimulating event of the day, aside from the arrival of food, was the spot of light from Sun Boy's torch. It started high on the wall, crawled downward and across the floor, then up the opposite wall before narrowing into nothing just before the time of darkness began.

Owl felt himself growing weaker from inactivity, and started to pace the confines of the lodge to remain strong. He must be able to escape when the time came. The other prisoners seemed to resent these efforts on his part, grudgingly moving aside for his pacing.

At first none would communicate at all. Finally the old man, who had first answered the hand signs, condescended to at least acknowledge Owl's queries. This, however, was not much better than nothing. He soon realized that the man was deranged. The evil spirit in him would sometimes make him giggle senselessly, though at other times he seemed almost rational.

It was during one of the more sensible periods that Owl managed to communicate at some length with him. The Old Man, as Owl thought of him, was apparently not so old, though his hair was white. He had no idea how long he had been a prisoner. Had he ever tried escape? Of course, at first.

Owl could not understand the man's attempts to tell him his tribe. It was one unfamiliar to the People.

Owl was puzzled. Surely the man's entire captivity had not been spent in this lodge. Efforts for further information on this point were fruitless, answered only by a vague hand gesture toward the southwest. Another puzzling circumstance bothered him even more. For what purpose would one hold another person in captivity? He attempted to question the Old Man.

"What will be done with us next?" he signed.

"They will sell us," came the quick answer, "to the Hairfaces."

A look of apprehension crept over the sallow face, and the man began to jabber quietly. The spirit was bothering him again, Owl saw, and ceased his questioning. The other wandered over against the wall, sank to a recumbent position, and curled up like a child, whimpering softly to himself.

Owl was touched by the pitiable sight, but also had much to think about. "The Hairfaces!" What could be meant by that? The only man he had ever seen with fur upon his face was his father. Could it be possible that the people of whom the Old Man spoke with such dread were the tribe of Owl's father? If so, he would undoubtedly be welcomed when he identified himself. He settled back against his own section of the wall, almost elated. This could be the solution to all his problems, to find his father's people.

Still, gnawing at the back of his mind, was the memory of the Old Man's inordinate dread of these people. And what, he wondered uneasily, had turned his hair prematurely white?

Owl's natural optimism won out, and he decided that his own case was considerably different from that of the Old Man. Adding to his anticipation was another sign of good medicine. As the twilight deepened, he heard a coyote's call from the far hilltop.

By the time of the arrival of the Hairfaces, Owl had managed to convince himself that this was to be an event of extreme good fortune. It was with actual anticipation that he climbed the ladder with the other prisoners and stood blinking in the unfamiliar sunlight.

A glance toward the camp site near the creek showed him that the Head Splitters had long since departed. He felt a pang of loneliness. The tribe of his captors had been the last vestige of contact with his own people of the plains.

The slight twinge of regret was immediately overshadowed by interest in that which was new. Below him in the path between the lodges were several men on horses, moving at a leisurely pace toward the center of the village.

The man who appeared to be their leader sat on a magnificent black stallion. He wore strange bright-colored garments and headgear, and a medicine shirt that Owl suddenly realized was exactly like one he had seen before. Over his parent's sleeping robes in the lodge far away hung an unused chain-mail shirt. Owl had grown up knowing only that it represented a part of his father's past heritage. It was considered strong medicine among the People, but Owl had never seen it worn.

The man on the black stallion rode past the lodge, and Owl, looking down directly on him, saw that this shirt was indeed like his father's. The slender curling strands shone glittering in the sunlight, and dull metallic sounds emanated from the rider as he moved.

With a thrill of excitement, Owl saw that the men on horses, and many of those on the ground, did indeed have fur upon their faces. One man, riding directly behind the leader, glanced up, and the astonished Owl saw that he greatly resembled his father. Certainly closely enough to have been a relative. Perhaps, Owl pondered, the Hairface could even be my uncle! He could hardly wait for the coming confrontation.

How could he contrive to present the most impressive scene? His mind raced ahead. He remembered well the techniques of White Buffalo, and how the old medicine man could milk the last drop of drama out of a situation.

Owl had only a moment to plan his scene, however. The last of the procession passed below, and their captors motioned the prisoners to descend the ladder to the ground. They were shoved roughly forward in the direction the Hairfaces had taken.

The horsemen had dismounted and were facing an open area, awaiting the approaching file of prisoners. The captives were led forward, and by sign language, one of the Mud Lodge people indicated that they were to kneel. The men on either side dropped woodenly to their knees. Now, thought Owl, now is the time. He drew himself to the full height of his young manhood, and addressed the leader of the group, using hand signs.

"I am Owl," he began, "son of Heads Off, chief of the Elk-dog band of the People. My father is a Hairface, of your tribe! I am of your people!"

All eyes were on him, astonished at his revelation. Owl stood, smiling and expectant, waiting for the welcoming answer from the Hairface leader. He was still smiling when the whip struck across his bare shoulders, each of the metal-tipped lashes raking a thin strip of skin. Owl screamed, and dropped writhing to the ground, still crying out in pain. The Hairface leader smiled thinly.

Three more times the whip hissed through the air, the burning cut of the multiple lashes searching, wrapping, stripping skin. Finally the punishment stopped, and there was silence for a moment, broken only by the delirious giggle of the demented Old Man.

A couple of the Hairfaces moved among the prisoners, tying them together by means of a rope knotted around each left ankle. Their leader stalked over to his horse and stepped nimbly up. He reined the animal around, then turned and spoke to the man with the whip.

"Bring them along," he said casually. He pointed with his quirt at the prostrate figure on the ground. "If the half-breed bastard makes trouble, give him another taste of the cat!"

The tongue of the Hairfaces was completely foreign to Owl, but the meaning was clear. He glanced over at the man with the whip, intending to remember his appearance for future use. The stern glare he encountered made him drop his eyes again as he painfully rose with the others and shuffled after the riders.

So these were men of his father's tribe. No wonder he had left them to join the People.

10

During his previous captivity, Owl had attempted to adjust to the circumstances. Now his predicament was not to adjust, but to survive. Any slight deviation from the expected brought an instant shouted curse and a stroke of the whip.

This instrument was several paces in length, and it became apparent that it could be used with great accuracy. For some reason which was obscure at first, it was called *"el gato"* in the language of the Hairfaces. It was learned that this phrase meant "the cat," and the meaning became more apparent. A prisoner subjected to a stroke of the whip would exhibit a series of deep parallel cuts in the skin which resembled the claw marks of a giant cat.

It did not take Owl long to recognize the origin of the odd crisscross scars on the back of the Old Man.

The overseers ordinarily carried the whip coiled in the right hand, looking for all the world like a braided rope or a great black snake. It was easy to glance at the coils and wonder how many hapless prisoners had contributed the color of their blood to the greasy hue of the device. The butt of the whip, nearly as thick as one's wrist, was held by a thong looped around the forearm of the overseer.

There were several of these men, charged with management of the prisoners. One stood out above all others, however, for his sadism. It was he who had initiated Owl to the bite of *el gato* in the courtyard back in the village of the Mud Lodge people. At any pretext he sent the burning lash searching for tender skin with a vengeance. At times it seemed as though the man was actually disappointed if there were no infractions. The other overseers were content if the prisoners were quiet and cooperative, but this one wielder of the dreaded cat was constantly restless. It was thought that his pleasure in its application was so intense that he occasionally applied an unjustified blow just to pass the time.

He was of scarcely more than medium height, but very broad and muscular in the shoulders. His muscles were overdeveloped from wielding the cat, it was said. Perhaps this was true, for his lower body and legs were disproportionately slender. It was as if the man had been assembled from parts of two differently shaped individuals. His neck was short and thick, allowing his head to rest, it appeared, directly on his heavy shoulders. A fringe of beard straggled around the periphery of his face, framing a perpetual look of evil ill-temper. The small, close-set eyes wandered constantly, looking for the slightest excuse to unleash the cat. In no time at all the prisoners had applied to the man himself the name of his favorite instrument. He was El Gato.

He seemed to take special delight in watching for any infractions on the part of Owl. It became a one-sided game, with all the rules favoring the man with the whip. Owl was unsure why he had been singled out for special attention. He realized, however, it must have been because of his outburst back in the village. How utterly stupid of him, he now reflected. He had actually expected the Hair-faces to welcome him into the hospitality of their tribe. Yes, it had been a serious mistake to draw attention to himself. Now, it was apparent that the primary objective of every prisoner should be not to catch the attention of the overseer. It was much better to become only one more of the faceless, dull entities, part of the sameness that was the mark of the captives.

There were perhaps as many prisoners as there are days in a moon. Owl was still puzzled as to why the Hairfaces kept this group of captives huddled in subjugation. They eagerly looked forward to one bright spot in the day, the distribution of the poor-quality food. Occasionally the guards would come into the mud-walled enclosure and single out a handful of the captives for some menial task, such as carrying sacks of grain or logs of firewood.

Downtrodden and low in spirit as he was, Owl still had one faculty over which he had very little control. His strict training under the medicine man had so deeply ingrained the habit of observation that he gathered information without consciously doing so. In this way he gained much knowledge of the Hairfaces on the infrequent occasions when he was among those chosen for the work party.

There were several things about his captors which Owl found almost beyond belief. He had already noticed, on the punishing march from the mud-hut village, that they made extensive use of the shiny medicine material. His father had a small knife of this sort, in contrast to the flint blades and spear points made by old Stone Breaker of the People. His father's elk-dog medicine, in fact, the jingling thing that enabled control of the horse, was formed of the shiny stuff. Now, he saw that the material was used by the Hairfaces for many things. All of their elk-dogs wore the medicine objects in their mouths. Several of the men had medicine shirts like that of his father, formed of tiny links of the substance. Some of their chiefs carried long, shiny knives, as long as one's arm, which again, he thought, must be similarly made. *Aiee,* with so much strong medicine, the Hairfaces must be undefeatable.

He became certain of this a few days later. A ceremony was held at which a demonstration of the powerful medicine of the Hairfaces was carried out. The prisoners were allowed to watch.

A group of men dressed alike, and with the demeanor of warriors brought forth a strange object from one of the lodges. It was pulled on wheels, like those of the carts used to carry firewood and grain. Owl had become used to the wheels, another wondrous evidence of the medicine of the Hairfaces. He had wondered how to attempt to describe these marvels to the People on his return.

Now, the warriors were dragging the heavy object on a two-wheeled cart. It appeared to resemble a section of hollow log about two paces long, except that it was made of the shiny substance that the Hairfaces used for so many of their medicine things.

The men dragged the thing into position and turned it so that the log pointed away from the lodges. With great ceremony a quantity of black sand was poured into the log, followed by what appeared to be a piece of a grain sack. This was pushed down the log with a pole, and a round boulder selected from a nearby pile. This was found to exactly fit the hole in the log. It, too, was pushed in with the pole.

Owl was thoroughly confused. He would have thought the Hairfaces had become completely demented, except that he had become convinced that they did nothing without some reason.

The warriors stepped back. One advanced cautiously and applied a burning torch to a spot on the top of the log. There was a blinding flash and a thunderous roar. White smoke billowed from the log. Before Owl's astonished eyes, a large boulder several hundred paces across the valley exploded into innumerable small pieces and disappeared. Echoes of the blast reverberated across the hills, then it was quiet except for the delirious giggle of the Old Man. As the dust and smoke settled, the warriors prepared the smoke-log for another burst.

Several times the deafening roar was repeated. Some of the prisoners held hands over their ears, while others cried out in terror.

Owl's astonishment did not prevent him from noticing the really important fact. The smoke-log would make it possible for the Hairfaces to destroy an enemy at a distance of several hundred paces.

And, if their medicine could reach over great distances, how could they be beaten? More to the point, it might be that escape was entirely impossible. How could one escape medicine so powerful?

That night Owl was more depressed than at any time previously. He had begun to think perhaps the Old Man was right.

"From the Hairfaces," he had said, "there is no escape."

11

Several suns after the smoke-log demonstration Owl discovered, among the prisoners already with the Hairfaces, another man of his own tribe. The man was somewhat older than himself, and had been among the Hairfaces for several winters.

Owl discovered him accidentally. It was meal time, and the guards had brought a kettle of the ever-present stewed corn. The prisoners filed past, and a man ladled a scoop of the substance into each bowl.

"Aiee" murmured a voice behind Owl. "Corn soup again." The man spoke as if to himself, but Owl had been thinking the same thing. And, he realized suddenly, in the same language. This must be a man of the People!

The two walked over against the wall of the compound, and Owl squatted beside the other. They ate in silence for a short while and then Owl initiated a conversation, using the People's tongue.

"It is much different from well-cooked hump ribs," he observed cautiously.

From his attempts at communication with the crazed Old Man, he had become wary. The Old Man, when approached unexpectedly or too rapidly, would retreat into his own confused world, and babble to the spirits which possessed him, sometimes for hours. Owl had become very cautious about approaching other prisoners too abruptly.

There was a long silence, then the other man finally spoke softly.

"You are of the People?" he asked timidly. Owl nodded eagerly.

"I am Owl, son of Heads Off, of the Elk-dog band."

"And I am, or was, of the Red Rocks. My name, Long Bow." He formed the words hesitantly, from long disuse.

"Have there been others of the People here?" Owl pressed.

"Oh, yes, my friend. Most have been killed trying to escape."

"Have you tried?"

"Of course. It brought me this the last time." He held his right hand forward, fingers spread. There was no thumb.

The significance sank through to Owl. Without a right thumb one could not handle weapons. Enough to hunt, perhaps, although clumsily, but not with enough proficiency to engage in combat. Or, to escape, Owl realized. One would need every skill to escape from the Hairfaces' strong medicine.

"I can still carry the sacks," continued Long Bow, smiling in grim humor. Owl was later to realize the significance of the remark.

The two talked a long while. It was pleasant to hear one's own tongue again. Long Bow had been stolen from the Red Rocks band when a young man. The Head Splitters had kept him for one winter, and then traded him to the Mud Lodge people. They had in turn sold him to the Hairfaces. There had been several of the young People originally, now all dead. He had seen two of them killed in escape attempts, and the others never returned. The Hairfaces always announced to the other prisoners that the fugitives had been killed.

"Just as I would do," Owl nodded. Perhaps escape was possible, and their captors concealed any such successful attempts.

"No," Long Bow shook his head, "I think not. The Old Man," he gestured at the pitiful babbling creature, "has escaped many times. He is always caught by the Mud Lodge people or someone, and brought back."

Still, Owl thought it possible that there were escapees unaccounted for. His spirits rose a little.

He told Long Bow of his initial encounter with their captors, and his expectation of welcome into their tribe. The other man's mouth dropped open in shocked horror.

"That is why El Gato has a special hate for you," he mused. "Of course! To them, you are a half-breed." He glanced around apprehensively. "I think El Gato is probably of mixed blood." He hesitated again. "You will understand, my friend, if I do not wish to be seen with you too much?" He edged away and sat down some distance from Owl.

Nevertheless, they occasionally found opportunity to talk. Owl brought the other the general news of the People since the time of Long Bow's capture. He already knew of the death of Hump Ribs, chief of the Elk-dog band, in the Great Battle, but it was shortly after that he had been captured. Was old Many Robes, real-chief of all the bands of the People, still alive?

"Oh, yes," Owl assured him, "he goes on and on. He was old when my father first came to the People."

Long Bow nodded. "Is there talk of who might be the next real-chief?"

Owl shook his head. "I think the People are happy and

rich enough since the Great Battle, they do not worry about who is real-chief. I had heard nothing, at least until I left." He explained the circumstances of his departure, now over a year ago, and his quest for the medicine vision.

"*Aiee,* you are a medicine man? It is bad that you should come to this!"

"It is bad, my friend, that *anyone* should come to this," Owl answered firmly.

Long Bow was able to give much information about the purpose of their captivity. This was, he informed Owl, a seasonal lull in their activity. Cold Maker, though not so powerful here as at home, was unpredictable. The Hairfaces did not like to be in the mountains during winter, so they retreated to this place, bringing the prisoners. Here they waited until the Greening Moon, or—the man hesitated.

"Owl, I have lost count of the moons, they are so different here." He shook his head. "No matter. They will take us again to the mountains."

At this point, he used words unfamiliar to Owl, and the young man again lost the line of the conversation. He stopped the speaker again.

"But *why?* What purpose does this have?"

"To carry the rocks," answered Long Bow, a little irritably. Then he explained, a bit more patiently. "We dig the yellow rocks from a hole in the mountain, and carry the sacks down to the *arristra.*" Another unknown word, Owl reflected. Perhaps he would understand when he saw the place.

"Why do they want the rocks?"

"For the shiny medicine stuff in them!" the exasperated Long Bow burst out.

Suddenly, the truth about the Hairfaces, their presence here, their reasons for holding the prisoners, all began to become clear to Owl. The pieces fit together.

He had noticed that there were two kinds of the shiny

medicine. The more common sort, that which their weapons were made of, was whitish, like the shiny sides of the small fish in the streams. The other, this yellow kind of which Long Bow spoke, seemed more highly regarded by the Hairfaces. They appeared to have almost a reverence for it. Could it be, he marveled, that this yellow stuff which glittered was even stronger medicine than that which made the smoke-log roar?

12

With the new information as to the Hairfaces' intent and purpose came new understanding. Old White Buffalo had continually urged his young apprentice to look beyond, to see why, to learn how all things relate.

Now Owl could see more clearly the position of the Mud Lodge people. The Hairfaces must have men to dig and carry the shiny medicine rocks. If they did not have the men they needed, they would find them. The nearest tribes, those of the Mud Lodges, would be forced to dig and carry, unless they could furnish prisoners for that purpose.

This new understanding did not prevent Owl's ill will toward both groups. It simply was comforting to him to realize that there was some reason left in a world which had seemed completely mad.

In one area of the Hairfaces' medicine, however, he was still completely baffled. That was their medicine man. Owl had identified the man early in his captivity. He knew this must be a medicine man because his garments were different. The other Hairfaces showed a great deal of respect for the man, also.

He was short, somewhat fat, and wore a robe that reached nearly to the ground. There were several objects made of the shiny yellow medicine rock that dangled around his neck and waist. The medicine man constantly handled the beads on one of these thongs, sometimes murmuring a chant under his breath. His chants were highly regarded by the other Hairfaces. More than once Owl had seen an individual stop and lower his head while the medicine man made gestures over him, sometimes with a short chant.

This man was the only Hairface who did not actually have facial fur. For a time Owl wondered if this had some meaning, but finally decided not. Other Hairfaces had varying amounts, seemingly independent of their status and power.

Owl did puzzle considerably over the medicine symbols used by the man. One constantly recurred, in the objects hanging around his neck, and was stitched on the front of his garment. It consisted of an upright portion, which appeared to be connected to a shorter cross member. This design held very great significance for all the Hairfaces, but was apparently under exclusive control of the medicine man. He obviously held the symbol in great reverence. Once he was seen to take the dangling example around his neck and touch it to his mouth in a kiss. This, no doubt, rejuvenated his powers, Owl decided.

The same symbol, which now appeared to Owl the most powerful medicine of all, was seen in one more prominent place. In the center of the Hairfaces' village, among the cluster of dwellings, stood the medicine lodge. The lodges were all similar to those of the Mud Lodge people, squarish and flat topped. But these of the Hairfaces had large square doorways, through which a man could walk upright. These openings could be shut with a flat device made of wood, instead of skins. They hung from one side of the opening, rather than from above.

But in the midst of the cluster of these curious dwellings was the medicine lodge. It was easily the tallest man-made structure Owl had ever seen, towering high above the ground. It would be as tall as several men standing on each others' shoulders, and was magnificent in appearance. Decorative designs in stone adorned this lodge, and on the top of the highest point of the structure was yet another symbol. It was the same as the emblem so revered by the medicine man, but in a greatly enlarged form.

The upright was formed of a log as thick as one's thigh, fixed firmly in the solid sun-baked mud of the medicine lodge. Lashed tightly to this was the second log, equally massive, and greater than the span of a man's arms. There remained the mystery of the symbolism of this device, but it was obvious that it was a very potent force in the customs of the Hairfaces. Perhaps their greatest medicine, Owl thought.

He was puzzled. Why did his father, from this same tribe, not have this most powerful of medicines? It was generally assumed among the People that Heads Off possessed strong medicine, but it was different. It was elk-dog medicine, and related primarily to control, management, and training of horses.

Perhaps, Owl reasoned, this medicine of the tree was the exclusive property of the medicine man. Yes, that must be it. It would be like White Buffalo's knowledge of the herds, and the time of the firing of the grass. Like his own medicine, in fact, learned laboriously as the old man's assistant. Indeed, the medicine man of the Hairfaces seemed to have a couple of young apprentices who assisted him, especially in the area of the medicine lodge.

The big medicine lodge was unquestionably under the

sole authority of the medicine man. Under his direction, large numbers of the Hairfaces gathered periodically for a time. The voice of the medicine man could be heard, raised in chants and incantations, and occasionally, his listeners could be heard to respond in a short chant, also.

Owl longed to catch a glimpse inside. As the days dragged on, it became almost an obsession with him. He came to think that a brief look, an insight into the qualities of this most potent of medicines, was somehow his most important goal. Next to escape, of course. That remained his primary occupation, but had been postponed until the changing of the seasons. Still, Owl came to believe that many of the mysteries of all existence might be opened if he could only see inside the medicine lodge.

He spoke to Long Bow about it, and received an answering look of terror.

"I do not know, Owl, but I think it would be very dangerous. It is too powerful a medicine for us." He refused completely to talk about it any further.

Owl was inclined to discount Long Bow's fears. The use of a powerful medicine is only dependent on knowledge of it. Long Bow did not have expertise in such things. Besides, he had been a captive so long that his spirit was gone. He had become fearful.

Owl's opportunity to look into the secrets of the medicine lodge came quite by accident. It was in what must have been the Greening Moon, shortly before the prisoners were moved to the mountain. Owl was among a group of workers who had been unloading firewood from carts. Sun Boy was nearing the edge of the world and shadows were long as they shuffled back through the village to their enclosure. Their over-seer walked alongside, intent on watching for any infraction.

Just as they were opposite the medicine lodge, one of the Hairfaces called to the man with the whip, and the other stopped to converse with him. The prisoners, glad for any opportunity, began to slump to a squatting position of rest. Owl glanced at the preoccupied overseer, and took a few steps in the direction of the medicine lodge as he squatted.

From this position he could see through the massive doorway, which stood open. It took a moment to adjust his eyes to the dimness inside, but soon he could make out shapes and objects. Light came from the small fires burning on the tips of the lumps of fat used by the Hairfaces for this purpose. By this dim light he could see what originally appeared to be men and women in strange garments. Then he realized they were only effigies.

Suddenly he saw, at the far side of the medicine lodge, an effigy larger than all the others, and horrifying beyond belief. He hoped it was an effigy, though it could have been an actual person. At least, it was life-sized.

Against the far wall of the medicine lodge had been erected another of the symbolic trees. And, horribly impaled with stakes driven through hands and feet, hung the prisoner. He was clad only in a breechclout, and his head hung forward, in death or unconsciousness.

Owl crept cautiously back to the line of other prisoners. He could hardly comprehend the barbarity of this form of torture. *Aiee*, it was no wonder the medicine man commanded such respect. Owl resolved to stay as far from the man as possible.

He did not abandon his thoughts of escape, but he would have to be very careful. He had no desire to be the next prisoner to be staked to the tree for torture.

13

The trail to the mine was narrow and steep, crawling along the shoulder of the mountain. On the uphill side the slope was rough and broken, with scrubby junipers scattered in the few accessible areas of soil among the boulders. On the other side, dropping precipitously, the canyon stretched along the trail nearly its entire length.

The depth was breathtaking to Owl, raised in the gently rolling prairie. He had, at first, an almost irrational fear of the cliff, soon erased by the hard physical labor of the task required. Still, after many days of staggering up the narrow path, and returning, bent under a heavy ore sack, there remained the dread of the height. Whenever he looked down at the pointed tops of tall fir trees, dwarfed by distance, his bowel tightened and his equilibrium became disturbed for a moment. He tried not to look down often. This was easy, because the utmost attention was required not to make a misstep, especially on the descent.

On this leg of the journey the ore sack on one's shoulders made a top-heavy load, and balance was critical.

On the return trip, several times between dawn and dark, it was sometimes possible to look far off across the canyon. The opposite range of shining mountains rose on above them, while in the vast intervening space eagles flew and fluffy clouds drifted. Owl never became accustomed to the strange feeling of looking down on drifting clouds or soaring eagles.

These moments of wonder were fleeting, however. Stationed along the trail were the overseers, each with his ever-ready whip. If a prisoner stumbled or seemed to be malingering, the stroke of the cat followed without hesitation. El Gato, more malevolent than ever, could always be counted on to assume a post about halfway up the trail. It was a difficult part of the path at best, very narrow around the shoulder of the mountain. Here there was not room for two to pass on the trail, so it was sometimes necessary to wait for another to traverse the narrow spot. Unfortunately, El Gato's post overlooked this portion of the path. The man had selected as his own a huge boulder, several paces in length and taller than a man's reach. He would pace the distance of the boulder's flat top like his namesake, turning at each end, to constantly keep the prisoners in view, if not in reach of the long lash.

It was the most dreaded portion of each round trip. To the prisoners, it was a grim game, the object of which was to save one's strength to traverse this short passage as rapidly as possible. If one loitered too long in other areas, of course, the whips of other overseers came searching. Still, in the mind of each prisoner was the sure thought. No cat searched, bit, and cut the skin as severely as that of El Gato. To pass El Gato's rock safely was the most important point of each trip.

Owl was pleased about one thing. Because of his youth and the strength of his legs, he had been placed on the carrying crew. The others, the diggers, were those who could sit or crouch in the hole for many hours and chip away at the rocks. It required less strength, so many of the older or weaker prisoners were assigned there. One exception was the Old Man. His sinewy build seemed to contain an inexhaustible reserve of strength. Though he might at times be confused, mumbling to himself or chuckling insanely, his step on the trail was quick and sure.

Owl, thankful for the assignment in the open air and sunlight, felt glad for the Old Man, too. A prisoner who had tried escape as many times as the Old Man's reputation indicated must long for freedom. Owl could sympathize. He felt that he himself would soon go mad in the depths of the mine-hole. He longed to talk with the Old Man about his escapes, to ask the reason for his failures, and his theories on the possibility of success. Several times he attempted to initiate such a conversation, but each time the same result ensued: The Old Man would become suspicious, withdrew, and revert to the incoherent babbling of the deranged mind. His lapses into insanity seemed to become, if not more frequent, at least more sudden as the moons dragged along.

Owl had observed much about the digging of the medicine rocks. They seemed to come from only one or two areas of the mountain, he noticed. One hole had apparently yielded up its store of yellow rock, and was abandoned, like an empty eye socket in the face of the hill. The active source, that which they were now working, seemed to yield a good quality of the medicine stuff. At least, the Hairfaces were pleased as they conversed over samples of the ore from the mine-hole.

Sacks were carried from the hole by the antlike line of prisoners to a more level area along the sparkling stream and emptied in a pile near the *arristra*. This device was simply a round boulder, tethered to a stake in the smooth granite shelf of the stream bed. It could then be rolled in a circle, crushing pieces of ore beneath it. In the shallow groove, ground by countless revolutions of the stone, gathered the shiny yellow particles so dear to the Hairfaces. The unwanted portions of the ore stones were washed away by the trickling water of the stream.

Owl had no knowledge of what became of the yellow sparkles after they were retrieved and sacked in small leather pouches. He did not particularly care. He had begun to suspect that this medicine might be more harm than good. He had seen no benefits that would appear to justify the extensive effort involved. Aside from the keeping of prisoners and the full-time effort of all the overseers involved, there were those who operated the *arristra*. All this for only a few pinches each day of the yellow stuff, And, so far, he could see not much use for it. It did not appear to make the hunt any easier, and was not used in growing. *Aiee,* there was much about the Hairfaces that was difficult to understand. Perhaps, he thought, there is something about the yellow stuff that makes men mad.

He shifted his uncomfortable load and stepped carefully along the trail. Ahead of him, the leathery Old Man plodded along, mumbling to himself. He had spent much time near the yellow medicine, Owl mused, and was clearly mad.

In front of the Old Man was another prisoner, carrying his load of ore. Owl had watched the man all day. He was sick, coughing frequently, and seemed very weak as they climbed that morning. Still, he had managed to keep up throughout most of the day, though staggering. At the mine, waiting to fill his ore sack, the man had been racked with such a paroxysm of cough that he had sunk to his knees. The overseer had prodded him up again, but now, several paces ahead of the Old Man, the prisoner seemed about to collapse.

Unfortunately, they were approaching the rock of El Gato when the man stumbled and fell. His precious ore sack pitched forward, struck the edge of the path, and bounced over the rim.

El Gato's roar of rage and cutting bite of the lash reached the prostrate form at almost the same instant. The man's shoulders twitched convulsively with the first few blows, then remained quiet. El Gato continued to curse and lash the unconscious form. Each stroke opened new cuts across the man's back, but he lay senseless on his face. The other prisoners remained still, fearing that the wrath of El Gato over the loss of the ore sack would extend to them also.

An overseer near Owl stepped past and trotted down the trail, squeezing past the Old Man. He spoke to El Gato and held a hand up to dissuade him for a moment. The Hair-face stepped over to the prone figure and lifted the head by the hair with one hand.

"Esta muerto!" he called to El Gato, letting the dead face drop back into the dust. El Gato shrugged and coiled his whip. The other man straightened, placed his foot against the dead prisoner, and gave a shove, rolling the body over the edge. He stood and watched it bounce down the cliff side and out of sight far below.

Owl's attention was suddenly caught by a movement on the part of the Old Man. They had dropped their ore sacks to the trail to rest for a moment while awaiting developments. Now the Old Man very carefully and deliberately picked up his sack, swung it in a long arc, and pitched it out into the canyon. He stood watching it fall, growing smaller and smaller below. The overseer was running toward him, readying his whip, and El Gato leaped from his perch and followed, eager to be in on the punishment.

The Old Man seemed perfectly calm as he stood and waited. He did not cower, but stood proudly, not even deigning to look at his captors. Just before they reached him, he suddenly lifted his head and started to sing. Without even turning his head, he stepped calmly off the edge, and followed the path of the falling ore sack. At Owl's last glimpse, the Old Man's song still drifted upward.

Owl stood in the dust of the trail, stunned. The Old Man had seemed perfectly rational. His was not a crazed, deranged shout as he went over the edge. It had been a completely deliberate action. The song, Owl realized, must have been the Death Song of the Old Man's tribe, in his own tongue.

He picked up his ore sack and plodded on down the mountain. The words of the People's Death Song came to him.

> The grass and the sky go on forever,
> But today is a god day to die.

Not for me, Old Man, he thought. In battle or in defense, but not that way.

Long Bow met him on the trail before he reached the *arristra*.

"What happened above?" he asked Owl as they passed.

There was no time for lengthy answers. Owl took a deep breath.

"The Old Man escaped," he said.

14

The death of the Old Man seemed to make little difference to the Hairfaces, but it had a profound effect on Owl. For a few suns he brooded. He became more homesick than at any time since his abduction so long ago.

He would dream at night that he was a boy in his parents' lodge again, and the fire would be burning low, and he was cold. Then he would wake and the low-burning fire would be the one around which the prisoners huddled for warmth. He would creep closer and attempt to get back to sleep.

Dreams of food also plagued him. How long, how long, since he had eaten crisp morsels of back-fat, or a slab of well-browned hump ribs. He remembered the morsels of raw liver eaten by the women during the butchering of buffalo. How desirable such a mouthful would now seem, after a diet of poor-quality stewed corn, beans, and dried pumpkin.

But most of all, his dreams of Willow tormented him.

Sometimes in half-waking confusion he could almost believe she had been entirely a dream. In his waking moments her memory was real enough. He relived a hundred times the ecstasy of their all too short one night together, and the bitter helplessness of seeing her clubbed down in her attempt to save him.

In his dreams, too, she was real. He could feel her soft body, the strong young arms around his neck. He tasted the warmth of her lips as she came to him. Then, awaking, his senses would doubt sometimes if Willow had ever existed, except as a beautiful dream.

Still, it was the memory of the girl that stimulated him to think again in terms of escape. She had always refused completely to accept the reality of captivity. She *would* escape. He had just dreamed one night the same dream of their escape, but this time awoke before their recapture. He awoke confused, but with the escape idea still foremost in his mind.

Shock had prevented him from adequately planning escape for a time, but now he was able to return to such thought. And, strangely, the incident of the Old Man's death had become the focus of his plans. He had noticed that, in the excitement of the moment, the overseers had become very careless in their watching of the prisoners. And El Gato, blind with rage, had become oblivious to all else.

Owl did not tell anyone of his thoughts, even Long Bow. It was not distrust of the man, but more like distrust of his lack of spirit. Owl still hoped to include Long Bow in the escape when the chance came.

There was one other major factor. Owl had no clear idea of how the attempt would happen. He only knew that when the time came, he would know.

By the time the chance occurred, the days were growing short. The prisoners were telling each other that soon it would be time to stop the gathering of medicine rocks.

There was ice on the edges of the calmer pools in the stream each morning.

These things lent a sense of urgency to Owl's thoughts. He was almost ready to concede that he must postpone escape until after the winter. Yet, he had decided, although he probably did not realize it, that this season must be the one. He *had* to make the try, and soon. The exact mode of his attempt refused to become clear in his mind.

He was making his way down the trail with a loaded ore sack when the solution came to him. There was the spot, he noted, looking ahead, where the sick prisoner fell. That had precipitated the wrath of El Gato, and the rest of the episode. Suddenly the answer was clear.

Owl carefully avoided any suspicious actions as he hurried past El Gato's rock, but he noted certain features of the trail. Again, on the return trip, he examined the rock and its overhang, taking care not to pause too long. His effort must take place on the last round trip of the day, or nearly so. He rehearsed the event in his mind on each journey past the rock. His actions must be timed exactly right, and must not arouse suspicion. He took one other step. Owl managed to work adjacent to Long Bow for the rest of the day, but still said nothing to him.

When the shadows from Sun Boy's torch began to grow long on the mountain, Owl decided this was the time. On the next carry down the trail he would make his try. Long Bow was behind him as he started the walk that would be, one way or another, his last on the mine trail.

El Gato recognized him and watched him carefully down the path. Owl staggered a little, and Long Bow called out from behind to ask if he were sick. Owl did not answer. This must be very convincing. As he neared the rock, under the watchful eye of El Gato, the stagger became worse. When he fell, it was nearly at the same place where the unfortunate prisoner had died.

Owl sagged to his knees and pitched forward. His ore

sack tumbled to the path. It had been a temptation to let it slip over the edge, but he had rejected that approach. The episode must be somewhat subtle.

The roared curse of El Gato reached his ears, and Owl knew that the cutting lash would follow. He covered his head with his arms for protection and allowed the first stroke to fall. Then, screaming and bleeding, he rolled and scrambled toward the overhang of the rock. Once more the lash struck across his hips before he huddled against the smooth stone, whimpering and crying.

The mid-portion of the rock bulged somewhat, over-hanging the trail, and it was to this spot that Owl had scrambled. It was no protection at all. El Gato's whip could reach any spot along the path for many paces. To see this small area, however, El Gato must move to the uphill end of the rock and lean out over the trail. He did so, now, chuckling at the stupidity of the prisoner who sought shelter where there was none. The whip coiled and whistled through the air.

Suddenly the cowering prisoner under the rock was transformed. In an instant, just as the lash struck, strong brown hands grasped out, seizing the biting strands. He gave a powerful heave with muscles grown strong from lifting ore sacks. El Gato felt the pull on the whip, and, in his leaning position, was suddenly overbalanced. He released his grip to free himself from the danger, but the deadly instrument was tied firmly to his wrist by the thongs.

Slowly, the massive bulk of the man tipped forward over the rock, across the trail and into the canyon. Owl had the satisfaction of looking directly into the face of El Gato. At only a little more than arm's length, he saw the brutal, sadistic expression change to one of stark terror. El Gato did not scream. There was only a short choking gasp of disbelief as he launched into the void.

For a moment it looked as if El Gato would attempt to fly. He spread his arms wide, grasping at nothingness, and seemed to hover like the eagle when she leaves her nest. Then he plummeted downward. Owl crouched on the narrow shelf, watching fascinated as the man's body disappeared among the fir tips far below. His last glimpse was of the whip, still tied fast and trailing behind, waving straight upward in the wind of El Gato's passing.

"Run!" shouted Long Bow. "El Gato is dead!"

Prisoners began to scatter up the slope, and Owl darted around the rock and joined in the escape.

"El Gato esta muerto!" came the cry from another overseer, echoing in his own tongue the observation of Long Bow.

Some of the prisoners, too broken in spirit to make the attempt, simply cowered beside the trail. At least a dozen men, however, were sprinting upward, leaping from one boulder to another, putting distance between themselves and the Hairfaces. As he ran, Owl was puzzled for a moment. The overseers were not running in pursuit. He had just begun to wonder at this strange situation when the smoke-log boomed from the meadow below.

The entire slope was raked with scatter shot. Grape-sized pellets bounced and rattled among the boulders like hailstones. A juniper just ahead of Owl jerked and shuddered from impact, and needles scattered on the sand. Behind him, men screamed and fell bleeding, or continued to run, howling and limping.

Below, the officer barked orders and the cannon was readied again, a fresh cannister of shot rammed home. Again the slope was raked by death.

Owl continued to run and climb. He had some inkling that there must be limitations to the reach of the smoke-log. He did not know how far its medicine might reach, but he had noticed that there was a limitation in height. The smoke-log had always been used in a horizontal position. In addition, he was very much aware that the heavy device could not be moved over steep or rough ground.

The smoke-log boomed again, but this time the rattle of the missiles was behind him. He continued to run, panting now in the thin mountain air. The crest of the ridge was now only a long bow shot above him.

Lungs burning, he climbed the last few paces and stood looking back. Far below, antlike figures still scurried about, and distant shouts reached his ears. A white puff from the smoke-log drifted slowly over the expanse of the canyon, hanging over the abyss. A few heartbeats later the dull boom reached his ears.

The realization slowly dawned on him, and he felt like shouting in triumph. An eagle swept past on fixed wings, and Owl spoke to the bird.

"My friend," he muttered, tears coursing down his face, "I am as free as you are."

15

Far below, the Hairfaces moved along the trail and up the slope. Recaptured prisoners were herded together and toward the encampment in the meadow. A few men moved among the wounded, methodically clubbing those injured too severely to recover and be of use.

Owl stood numbly watching, detached from the reality below. There was no apparent effort at pursuit, and he realized that perhaps they were unaware that one of the prisoners had actually been successful in escape. He peered through the lengthening shadows, looking for other escapees, but saw none. There was no sign of Long Bow. Owl had seen him at his elbow just before the smoke-log boomed, but not since. He waited a short while, then decided that the other had either been killed by the first blast of the smoke-log, or had escaped and was in hiding. He had not much hope, since the Hairfaces behaved as if they had nearly every prisoner accounted for.

It seemed likely, in fact, that there would be no pursuit. Owl had devised his attempt in the fading time of Sun Boy's torch. Now, it would soon be dark and darkness would be on the side of the fugitive. Still, it seemed prudent to take certain precautions. They would probably expect him to travel east, toward his own people.

With this in mind, Owl started north, following the backbone of the ridge at a distance-eating jog. He slowed only when the terrain was too rough, or the footing unsure. By full dark he was out of sight of the twinkling campfires below.

When twilight became too poor to travel safely, Owl stopped for a while. He drank deeply from a stream, and then curled against the sun-warmed southwest face of a granite slab. He would move on after moonrise improved visibility.

Owl had intended to sleep a short while, but found that he was far too excited. He tried to occupy the time by planning. There were many obstacles to be overcome. He was alone, without food, weapons, or clothing, except for his breechclout.

Water seemed no major problem, since in this part of the mountains were many small sparkling streams. More important was the threat of the weather. This must be, by the People's reckoning, the Ripening Moon. Soon following would come the Moon of Falling Leaves, and the Moon of Madness. From tradition, he knew that the seasons came earlier in the mountains. It was said that Cold Maker lived on a mountain top far to the north, and came down each autumn to the plains. He had no way of knowing when to expect Cold Maker in this strange land. He was certain of one thing, however. The prairies of his people were so far away that he could not reach them before winter. It would be necessary to face the onslaught of Cold Maker here, in the mountains.

Perhaps that would be not entirely bad. There were

innumerable hiding places among the rocks and trees of the area. The fugitive would be in jeopardy from the Hair-faces, from the Mud Lodge people, and, if he traveled eastward far enough, from the Head Splitters. None of these people, Owl believed, would be traveling in the mountains to any extent, during the moons of the Cold Maker.

He would travel, he decided, north and east, but careful to remain in rough enough country to provide shelter and concealment. Then, if he determined that there was actually no pursuit, he could select and prepare a shelter for the winter months.

The moon was rising now, red and just past full. Owl waited until the light grew stronger, and started on again. As he traveled, he realized, he must devise weapons, and secure food and garments. He had no doubts at all about his ability to accomplish this. In fact, Owl was so pleased with his situation that he was ready to burst into song at any time. When the laughing call of his medicine animal, the coyote, came echoing across the canyon, the relief of tension was too much. He stopped, threw back his head, and yodeled back an answer for pure joy of being alive and free.

When daylight came he saw beaver ponds below him, and turned down the slope. The animals had been cutting in a stand of cottonwoods, dragging brush for their dams and to store for winter under the ice. Owl searched for some time before he found the object that he needed. A piece of cottonwood, cut cleanly at the ends by the beavers. It was slightly shorter than his arm, and in diameter somewhat less than his wrist. He hefted the club and found that it balanced well.

It had been years since he had used a throwing stick, but the familiar feel brought his muscles into coordination. Owl flung the stick with a full-armed sweep at a stump a few paces away, and was pleased at the accuracy of the throw. It bounced off with a hollow thunk and he stepped over to retrieve it.

Now he was armed. True, it was with a childish weapon, used mostly among the People for the amusement of children. Still, the throwing stick could be effective. Most families of the People welcomed the addition to their food supply which small game provided. This was also a matter of prestige among the young. The first kill of nearly every hunter was a fat rabbit, knocked over with the thrown stick. This could lead to a great deal of honor among one's peers in the Rabbit Society.

So, with a great deal of confidence, Owl continued his journey. He had managed to find another well-balanced stick in case he lost one.

Returning to the ridge, he spent some time on a high rock, searching the entire area. There was no sign of pursuit, and he began to relax on that score. He must still be watchful, but immediate danger seemed minimal. He evaluated the landscape to better formulate his plans. Blue ridges, one beyond another, could be seen in all directions. It was obvious that the higher, snow-capped ranges were to the west, but there were many days' travel of rough country anywhere he looked. Owl was pleased to see no smoke in the still morning air. It would be very unlikely that anyone in these mountains would be anything but dangerous to him.

Perhaps two days' distance to the northeast lay an area of rough broken ridges covered with a heavy growth of pine and fir. It was not the sort of locale in which a group of people would spend a winter. That was exactly what made Owl consider it ideal for one lone fugitive. It lay in his direction of travel anyway.

Behind him a jay scolded, and he dropped quickly to his belly to peer over the rock's edge. It was only a doe and her half-grown fawn, stepping daintily across the ridge. Owl watched them out of sight, needing the food, shelter and clothing they represented. He must wait, though, for that sort of kill, until he could contrive better weapons. He rose and traveled on.

Two more stops he made that day. The first was to investigate a rocky outcrop below the crest of the ridge. He was delighted to find that the formation of white stone contained a vein of the substance he sought. It was a good grade of flint. With another stone he battered at the blue-gray streak until he had a pile of chips from which to choose. He selected several good-sized flakes, seeing in his mind's eye knives for cutting, spear points, and arrowheads. Owl was certainly not as skilled in the shaping of weapons as old Stone Breaker of the People, but he understood the principles involved.

The handful of sharp flint became clumsy to carry, and finally Owl discarded all but the best fragments. He removed his breechclout and used it to wrap a bundle of the remaining flints. The thong from his waist now held the packet with one of the throwing sticks over his shoulder as he started on.

The second stop was prompted by hunger. He observed a bear eating berries and turned aside to try them himself. White Buffalo had always impressed him with the fact that anything bears eat can be eaten by people. The berries grew in profusion along the stream, but were coarse and bitter, very unsatisfying to his empty stomach. In fact, he had not thought much of food until now, but began to have pangs of hunger, prompted by the abortive attempt.

He climbed back toward the better traveling on the ridge, and heard the chattering of a squirrel. He turned aside again, and soon saw several of the dark gray animals with long tufted ears, actively harvesting pine seeds. Owl picked up a cone, and pried a few seeds out to taste. They had a nutlike flavor, although they tasted strongly of the resin of the pine tree.

He decided this might provide sustenance, but his real

desire was for red meat. He had feared for some time that his teeth were loosening, and his gums were constantly sore. Clearly, his craving for meat must be satisfied. After several tries, he managed to knock over two of the fat squirrels. They were smaller than the fox squirrels in the canyons of his prairie country, but appeared acceptable fare.

Owl had decided that he could chance a fire, so he carried the squirrels and selected an open spot on the ridge. Carefully he chose dead twigs that would burn without much smoke. The light breeze would rapidly disperse that. Dried grass and a handful of cedar bark for tinder completed his preparations.

From the south exposure of a nearby slope he obtained a couple of dry yucca stems for rubbing sticks. His firebow was bent from a willow branch and strung with the thong from his breechclout. In a short while a fire was crackling while he skinned and cleaned the squirrels. The skins were carefully saved.

Owl found that the meat tasted of pine resin, probably due to the animal's diet. Still, when one's stomach needs meat, he reflected, who is to worry about the taste of a little pine?

He finished his meal and extinguished the fire before gathering his small store of belongings for travel. It had been a good day, Owl thought. He had started with absolutely nothing, and now had weapons, fire-making sticks, the necessary material for making more tools, and had eaten satisfactorily. Yes, the day had gone well.

As Sun Boy's torch slipped behind the snow-capped range to the west, Owl moved on, placing distance between him and the obliterated cooking fire.

16

The general area that Owl had observed as his immediate goal proved not two days' travel, but more than twice that. He was accustomed to estimating across grassland. The uneven, almost vertical nature of some of the terrain made travel much slower than he had anticipated. In addition, the illusion of nearness in the rarefied air was deceiving.

After the first day of travel Owl realized the error of his estimate and changed his plans somewhat. He would stop on high ground to observe his back trail, and spend a day or two in hunting and improving his weapons.

He was also becoming concerned about protection from the elements. So far the weather had been uncommonly fine, but he was apprehensive. Almost any day Cold Maker might whimsically unleash a puff of cold rain, sleet, or even snow. Owl had no desire to be caught with merely a breechclout to shelter his body. Not even that, for the moment, since he was using it as a carrying bundle.

He noticed some bleached and scattered bones to his right a few paces, and turned aside to investigate. The bones were apparently from a deer, and judging from their well-gnawed and scattered condition, had been there for many moons. Owl continued to search, however, and finally found the skull, partially hidden under a juniper bush. He was elated by the find. The animal had been a yearling buck, and the slender antlers, only as long as his finger, were exactly what he needed. With a small boulder, he succeeded in breaking the spikes from the skull. They would become tools for chipping flint.

Owl spent a time with his new find, experimentally chipping small flakes from one of the pieces of stone in his bundle. He had used the sharp edge of this flint as a makeshift knife to skin the squirrels, but now refined the shape. It was tempting to continue working with the flints, but hunger pangs told him he must seek food.

He was not so fortunate as on the previous day. Searching as he traveled, Owl saw hardly a living thing, except a soaring hawk. He ate a quantity of pine seeds, and a handful of the berries he had tried yesterday. Remembering the bears' habit of overturning dead logs looking for food, he tried that. He examined the fat white grubs underneath, and decided he was not that hungry yet. Still, he remembered the tales of the old medicine man. Long before Owl was born, before they had elk-dogs to help with the hunt, the People had frequently used these and similar items as survival food. He would keep that in mind, but for just now, he hoped for better fare.

As Sun Boy's torch sank lower, Owl sought a place to spend the night, a sheltered spot against the south face of a sun-warmed rock. Preferably a dark-colored stone, since it would attract and hold more of the warmth from the heavenly torch. He selected his location, and built a small fire before dark. He had no need for a fire, nothing to cook, but it warmed his body and cheered him considerably. It was odd, he thought, how the dancing flames from even a tiny fire could raise one's spirits. He lifted his voice in the short song of the medicine man to the departing Sun Boy, the Thanks-for-Fire song.

Owl was careful to extinguish the blaze before darkness came, so the firelight could not be seen. He did not believe he was pursued, but took no chances. As he warmed himself over the dying embers, he thought again how satisfying it had been to enjoy the Fire song. He had not realized until now how very much he had missed the small daily rituals of the medicine man. Survival had been the most important thing in his life for many moons.

Now, cold and hungry though he might be, he could again enjoy some of the niceties of a cultured existence. These were his thoughts as he drifted to sleep.

He awoke with a start. The moon had risen, and a thin light illuminated the hollow below him. Owl kept very still for a moment, unsure of what had awakened him. It had been a noise, below him in the sparse trees. His hand closed on this throwing stick as he listened intently. The rock at his back was still warm. He pressed against it, shivering slightly from anticipation as well as the chill of the night air.

The sound came again. A rustling, chewing sound, which now seemed to come from near the top of a pine tree little taller than his head. Owl relaxed somewhat. An animal small enough to climb a tree no bigger than that would not likely be dangerous. He move silently away from the rock, and circled the tree. Soon he could see the irregular shape against the sky. A porcupine, methodically girdling the bark from the young tree, turned to look at him.

Owl was elated. The animal would certainly be acceptable food, and should be easy to kill. The porcupine moved slowly, secure in the protection of its sharp quills.

It climbed down the tree and waddled across an open area, heading for cover and concealment.

Owl circled warily, cautious of the barbed quills, but wanting the confrontation in a place where he could swing his club. The animal paused, threatening, turning its spiked tail toward the enemy. The tail lashed back and forth. Owl came close and dodged in, evading the lashing quills as he struck. One good blow across the porcupine's head, then another to make sure.

He knew better than to risk his fingers trying to skin the spiny creature in the dark. It could wait until morning.

Now that the excitement was over, Owl realized that the weather had grown considerably colder. He shivered as he retreated to the shelter of his rock.

After spending some time in trying to warm himself against the now cooling stone surface, Owl made a momentous decision. He would be forced to relight his fire. This was a sheltered spot, not visible for any distance, and the moonlight would lessen the chance of anyone seeing the reflection. Besides, he attempted uneasily to reassure himself, surely no Hairfaces would be wandering the mountains to search in the middle of the time of darkness. Nor would any other people who might prove dangerous, he reasoned, although not entirely convinced. One thing was certain. If he died from exposure such decisions would be meaningless. He took out his rubbing sticks and started to rotate the spindle in its socket.

He blew the ember into flame and added tinder and small sticks. When the fire was crackling cheerfully, he made a circuit around the entire area. He was pleased that he could see very little reflection of the fire from only a short distance away. And, perhaps more importantly, he had seen no one else's fire. The Hairfaces, he had noticed, built big fires. This had, in fact, been a joke among the prisoners. Their captors built large fires, and thus must stand well back, remaining cold. One could be much more comfortable over a small, well-tended blaze.

Owl, seeing no sign of other human presence, returned to add a few more small sticks to his own fire. He decided to utilize the situation, and dragged the porcupine carcass to where the firelight would illuminate the skinning process. His newly shaped flint knife performed well on the tough hide, and soon the skinned and gutted carcass was roasting on a stick. By daylight Owl had eaten well and saved some meat for the day ahead.

He was tempted to save the sharp spines of the animal's tail. The women of the People used the dyed quills for ornamentation of garments and various other items. Owl knew little of such things, but knew that his mother had always carefully hoarded any such quills she was able to acquire. Finally, amused at his own attitude, he threw the spines away, After all, what can one decorate if he has nothing?

The skin of the animal he saved, as he prepared again to travel.

17

Owl had decided to travel on. There seemed to be little game in this immediate area anyway. He was badly in need of the skin of some large animal for shelter. A deer or elk, perhaps. He had seen deer at a little distance, but did not have the weapons for an attempt at a kill.

With this in mind, he kept a lookout for more beaver cuttings and before Sun Boy was overhead had selected a spear shaft. The sapling had been dropped by the beavers where it had been cut, probably to cut up later or drag away to the dam. Owl trimmed off leaves and small twigs, and then laboriously sawed the pole to length with his newly shaped knife.

He stopped early for the day, and built a fire to warm the earth where he would sleep. His major purpose for an early camp, however, was to complete his spear. He had been working on a spear point whenever he stopped, and it was now nearing completion.

Ideally, he realized, he should soak one of his skins in water and ashes to remove the hair, but this would take several days. His need for rawhide to bind the spear was more urgent. He compromised by cutting narrow strips from the skin of the porcupine and singeing the course hair over the fire.

Stone Breaker, the expert weapons maker of the Elk-dog band of the People, would have been amused at the makeshift spear. He would have agreed, however, that it was serviceable. The improvised binding was bulky and crude, but was secure, and would shrink even more tightly as it dried. Now Owl felt ready to try for a deer kill when opportunity offered.

He chewed the remaining meat of the porcupine as twi-light fell. It was still tough and tasted of pine, but filled the belly.

This night was warmer than the last, but Owl was glad to see the torch of Sun Boy once more. He must find some-thing today for shelter. Even with the fire cautiously burn-ing all night, he had become chilled to the bone.

The kill, when it came, was in a very unexpected fash-ion. Owl noticed magpies noisily fluttering and scream-ing around a clump of willows, and cautiously crept down to investigate. He could see nothing until, spear at the ready, he parted the leaves and peered into the thicket.

The carcass of an elk lay in the brush, partially covered with sticks and leaves. Hair bristled on the back of Owl's neck as he glanced anxiously around. He saw nothing, and ventured to look closer at the kill. To pull down an animal as big as an elk, the hunter must be the great bear with white-tipped fur, the real-bear. A cougar, too, might make this sort of kill, he thought.

On closer inspection, all the while warily on guard, he saw that the elk was an old cow, probably weakened by age or infirmity. The soft underparts had been eaten away. Owl circled until he found evidence of tracks, and at last identified the hunter. The footprints were those of the great cat.

He was in no immediate danger unless the cougar returned to find him at its kill. The kill was fresh, and Owl knew that the habit of the real-cat was to gorge immediately and then retire to sleep off the stupor. The sleeping place might be far away, and the cat might not return for a day or two. Perhaps not even then, if a convenient new kill offered elsewhere. Owl should be completely safe as he attempted to salvage what remained of the kill.

This did not prevent him from being uneasy. He dropped his bundle of assorted possessions and began to work as rapidly as possible. He had no desire to be here when the cougar returned. Desperately though he needed this kill, he had no intention of meeting a real-cat in hand to claw combat for possession of it. Therefore, his actions were quick and decisive.

Deftly he split the skin up the belly, and stripped it from the carcass. There were holes and cuts from the cat's claws, but it was basically intact. It was necessary to roll the carcass over to pull the skin from under. This Owl accomplished by using a foreleg as a lever. His experience in the butchering drudgery while a prisoner of the Head Splitters now stood him in good stead. As expertly as any woman of the People, he trimmed out the best remaining cuts, tossing them on the raw side of the freshly skinned hide. He gulped a few mouthfuls of liver as he worked, his body starved for the nutrition of good red meat.

When Owl had assembled all the meat he thought he could conveniently carry, he stripped out the sewing sinew from alongside the backbone. This white glistening band of fibrous tissue would be needed as he attempted to fashion his garments for winter. He tossed it and the various small articles he carried into the skin, and bundled the four legs together to make a pack. He swung it to his shoulder and rapidly left the scene.

The pack was heavy, but no heavier than an ore sack, and far softer. Owl was on top of the world as he jogged along, his deliberate pace putting distance behind him. Occasionally he glanced back to make sure he was not followed. If he could find an acceptable area for his camp and his fire, he could forget about the threat of the great cat. They were known to avoid fire.

Odd, he thought. He had hardly dared build a fire for fear of the Hairfaces. Now he hardly dared do without one for fear of the real-cat.

When he did stop, it was with plenty of daylight left. He could not search in the dark for firewood tonight. His first move was to lay in a good supply. He had selected a sheltered area near a flowing stream, with plenty of wood close at hand. A grassy meadow stretched before him, and an abrupt cliff behind. It seemed an ideally defensible position. This was good, for he expected to spend several days here. There was meat to cure, and the skin to process.

Again his experience in the women's work of the Head Splitters was helpful. The first night he had the shelter of the fresh elk skin, turned hair side toward him, but this was only a temporary expedient. Next day he began his work in earnest.

All day he worked. He cut meat in slender strips and draped them to dry over a rack of willow sticks. At every opportunity, however, he worked with the elk skin. He scraped fat and loose tissue from the inner surface. He selected a sapling near his camp and bent it over to form a rail for working on the hide. He would pull, scrape, and work the stiffening hide intermittently, while he performed other camp tasks.

Badly needed were moccasins. His feet had become toughened, but were now sore from traveling over rocks. And he would surely need protection for his feet in the winter. He remembered a method told him by White

Buffalo. It would produce not the well-designed plains moccasin of the People, but an acceptable substitute.

With this in mind, he had skinned out the hock section of each hind leg separately. He had cut the skin in a circle around the thigh, and without splitting it, had inverted it toward the foot, detaching it above the ankle. Now he examined the two sleeves he had created, still with the flesh side out. On one side of each was a well-defined bulge, formed by the protruding hock of the animal. Owl held one of the skins against his foot. Yes, it was as White Buffalo had said. The bulging portion of the hock would fit his own heel almost perfectly. He slipped the skin over his foot experimentally, hair side still in. It was necessary, he found, to slit the portion above his own ankle. This could be fastened with thongs. The loose skin beyond his toes he gathered and tied like the mouth of a bag, leaving plenty of room for shrinkage. This extra space, he believed, could also be stuffed with dried grass or fur for warmth when Cold Maker really struck.

He rose and walked around, feeling clumsy in his new footwear, but realizing the great protection they would offer. Now he must wear the moccasins most of the time while the skin dried, to preserve the shape.

A magpie sailed across the clearing and alighted on his meat-drying rack to peck at the strips. Owl waved his arms to scare the bird away. This promised to become a real problem. The gaudy black and white birds seemed without fear. They and the smaller jays of various sorts seemed determined to rob him of all his labors. He found that it was best to do most of his work with the skins while sitting almost within arm's length of the drying meat.

Once, striking out with a stick, he landed a lucky blow and knocked a magpie fluttering to the ground. Very much aware of all possibilities for food, Owl methodically plucked the bird. It was smaller than it looked with the feathers on, but formed a quite acceptable addition to his food supply. He propped it on a stick over the fire.

As he carefully nibbled the last shreds of meat from the bones, Owl was developing a general plan for his sustenance. He would avoid entirely the use of any of the elk meat as long as possible. It would be stored for the Moon of Snows and the Moon of Hunger. He thought that he could manage to obtain enough small creatures for his daily needs. Squirrels, porcupines, birds, had all proved useful already. Even the small striped squirrels like the one flitting among the rocks might help sustain him if necessary.

He was not likely to be so fortunate as to share a real-cat's kill very often, but that was a possibility. And, he should be able to make his own deer kill occasionally. He did need more skins before really cold weather.

Owl rolled over to expose a new portion of his body to the warmth of the fire, and drew the elk skin around him. He was pleased with his progress. He had come in contact with elements of nature completely foreign to his prairie culture, and had so far managed to adapt. White Buffalo would be proud of him. He looked forward to telling the old man of all the things he had seen and done. There were wondrous things to be learned beyond the land of the People.

He thought of Willow. She, too, would be proud. He longed to share with her the triumph of his escape, and of his lessons in survival among strange surroundings. She would be amused, he knew, at his story of robbing the real-cat's kill. She would laugh at his strange-looking moccasins.

Sleep came slowly. The girl's memory troubled his mind. She had been so vibrant, so radiantly alive, that his mind refused to accept her loss.

Even the reassuring call of a coyote from the ridge seemed at odds with reality.

18

Again Owl was wakened in the night by soft rustling noises, this time from the meadow. The moon had risen, and by its light he could detect motion in the grass. The creatures seemed small, and he laid aside his spear to pick up the throwing sticks.

Crouching, he made his way toward the grassy clearing, keeping to the shadows. To his surprise, the meadow seemed alive with scampering forms. Rabbits! He congratulated himself on accidentally locating his camp almost on top of the rabbits' meeting place. He knew of such areas, with a level open space to run and play, and adequate food supply for the creatures. There were at least as many hopping forms as one has fingers.

Another hunter shared interest in the rabbits' council. From a dead pine came the hunting call of a great owl. Instantly every rabbit froze in position. Owl used the moment of inaction to move quietly to better location. By using the owl's hollow cry to distract the animals, he could benefit in improved hunting. The long-ears started to move cautiously again. To his surprise, one began feeding only a few paces in front of him. The stick whirled, and a fluffy rabbit lay kicking in the grass.

He flitted forward, administered another blow, and glanced quickly around for new quarry. It was several moments before he spotted his prey, another fat long-ear contentedly nibbling a blade of the lush grass. The stick whirled again. This time the blow was not so sure. The stricken rabbit threshed around in the grass, squealing in distress. All the other animals fled into the woods or among the rocks. Owl sprang forward to prevent the escape of his prey.

Just as he was almost ready to reach forward and grasp the kicking animal, a shadow flitted across his path. On silent wings, the great owl swooped softly in front of him and snatched the rabbit. It was gone almost before the bird's human namesake realized what was occurring.

Owl was furious for a moment, then became amused. The game belonged to one hunter no more than another. Had he not done the same with the kill of the real-cat? After all, it was with the help of the great owl that he had secured the first rabbit. He picked up his throwing stick and hurried back to claim that kill. He turned and waved to the silhouette in the dead pine, elongated by the rabbit carcass dangling below.

"Thank you, my brother," he called, with a laugh.

The rabbit was large and fluffy, and of a kind not familiar to him. In the prairies and woods of his home, there were two long-ears. There was the large, tough and bony animal with a black tail, and the smaller, softer, white-tailed rabbit, much better for eating.

This rabbit was neither. It was heavy and meaty, and when daylight came, Owl could see that it was strangely mottled with white patches among the brown.

Each night thereafter, when the moon rose, Owl and his feathered counterpart shared the hunt. Some nights were totally unproductive, some produced a meal for the day. On one memorable night, he secured two fat rabbits in addition to one seized by his silent-winged hunting companion.

One other maneuver he learned during this period. He could imitate the call of the hunting owl to perfection. This sound could freeze all motion on the part of the long-ears, and enable him to maneuver for better position.

Finally came the night when he decided the meadow was hunted out. The great owl had already moved on to better hunting. The remaining long-ears had become so wary that at the slightest movement in the shadows they vanished. Besides, the waning moon no longer lighted the meadow satisfactorily for hunting.

Owl had begun to construct a robe from the rabbit fur. The skins had no strength, but much warmth. Clumsily and painstakingly he stitched the skins together with sinew. He had fashioned an awl from a rabbit bone, honed to a fine point on a stone. Already his furry cape was large enough to throw across his shoulders, and it became larger with each rabbit kill. Scraps of fur he stuffed into his moccasins.

When Owl left the Place of Rabbits to move on into the mountains he was much better equipped and provisioned. He had decided that there was to be no pursuit. Danger from enemies would be from a chance encounter. Therefore, if he watched carefully to observe any sign of human activity, he should find safety for the moons of the winter.

There remained the selection of a winter camp site. Owl was having a great deal of difficulty in relating his knowledge of needs for winter to this strange region. His experience was with skin lodges, erected at the south edge of a growth of timber, to shelter from the north blast of the Cold Maker.

His greatest problem was lack of knowledge of the area. He had no way of knowing how deep the snow, or how cold the nights would be.

It was to be assumed that lower areas would be more habitable. In the edge of the mountains, familiar to the People, it was realized that deer, elk, and the big-horned sheep came down from the taller peaks to winter in the lowlands. Owl's search, then, was for a sheltered valley or canyon, inaccessible to casual travelers, with a water supply, game, and an exposure to the south.

At times he despaired of finding a wintering site with all these qualifications. One he rejected for lack of water. Another was too conspicuous to any passer-by. The best site he found was finally rejected with regret, after he realized there was no sign of game in the area. He continued to travel in the generally northeast direction.

He almost decided to travel as rapidly as possible out of the mountains, hoping to find a tribe of friendly Growers with whom he could winter. This plan he finally rejected, also. He could not risk being caught in the open by Cold Maker, or blundering into a band of Head Splitters by mistake.

Owl was beginning to feel depressed, even desperate. His earlier confidence was hard to maintain through the chill of the lengthening nights. Maybe, he was forced to consider, there was good reason why the Hairfaces shunned the mountains in winter.

There had still been no winter storm. Several times dark clouds had gathered over the peaks of the high ranges to the west, but then dissipated. If at any time one of these threatening situations materialized, Owl would be in a very vulnerable position.

He remembered once, long ago, seeing an aging buffalo bull circled by wolves. The animals were patient, and there was no doubt about the eventual outcome. The bull could fend off the nipping, feinting attacks for a day or two, but eventually he would go down.

Tonight, in the depths of depression, Owl began to feel like the tired old bull. So far he had been successful in his bid for survival, but for how long? Tired, hungry, thirsty, and cold, as he built his fire, he really began to doubt himself. Perhaps captivity would be preferable to the end that seemed likely. He was proud of his bid for freedom, but what good had all his effort been if the end result was the same? Would he, like the buffalo bull, go down when Cold Maker, now only nipping at his heels, unleashed the final onslaught?

He chewed a little of his precious dried meat and rolled into his makeshift skins for the night, still cold and thirsty.

19

It was some time during the night that Owl's medicine coyote came to him in a dream. He had been restlessly tossing, the transparent visions shimmering and fading like mirages in the prairie sun. He saw again the miseries of captivity, the escape from the Head Splitters, the recapture, and the death of Willow. Then, she was still there, smiling sadly and sympathetically as he sweated under the ore sacks. Her gentle yet determined face encouraged him, as her memory always did. Again, she vanished, to be replaced by the cruel leer of El Gato. The overseer, too, now disappeared in a flash of fire from the smoke-log, and Owl was running, climbing, lungs bursting. Then he was tired, cold, and hungry, and sank down in despair to rest.

Just at this time in his vision, when depression was overwhelming, a coyote trotted into his dream. The animal approached and sat on its haunches near him, looking directly into his face. Owl recognized his medicine beast.

"Do not despair, my son," came the soft chortling voice. Owl looked at the coyote dully, without spirit.

"The answer is very near," continued the gentle chuckle.

Even in his dream state, Owl was irritated. He had given the escape his best effort, and now felt the weight of failure falling heavy on his shoulders. Worse, even, was the diminishing likelihood of his survival. And here was the completely inappropriate advice of the mystical dream coyote.

"Very close by," continued the voice. "You have only to think and look. I will be with you, my son."

The expression on the face of the dream beast was so compassionate that it was impossible to remain frustrated. Owl felt a warm, comfortable emotion spread over him, and he was reassured. He reached out a hand to touch the coyote, to retain the sense of closeness, and the animal vanished instantly. His hand came in contact with the smooth stone against which he camped. He was alone in the night beside the embers of his fire. One cannot touch a medicine animal.

Still, the feeling of close comfort persisted. Owl remained wide awake, his senses alert. He took small sticks and fanned the embers to blaze again, all the while pondering the meaning of the vision. The rest of the night was spent in meditation, sitting over the tiny fire with his rabbit fur robe wrapped around his shoulders.

He was puzzled about the cryptic message, "The answer is very near." Was this to indicate nearness to this place, or in the nearness of time? Owl was inclined to believe that both might be implied. At any rate, it could do no harm to remain here in waiting for a short while.

In addition, he was comfortable here. There was a peaceful lack of urgency in the place, and it was pleasant to be here. This was in direct contrast to his feeling for the place as he made camp the night before. It was strange how the message in his vision had changed his attitude. Where he had previously been anxious, depressed, and impatient, he was now relaxed and expectant.

Most of the day Owl spent near his fire, and mostly in thought. Activity did not, at this time, appear productive. Sun Boy carried his torch in its slow arc across the southern sky, and Owl was content to sit and appreciate its warmth.

There was still the quality of expectant waiting, and toward the end of the day, Owl began to wonder if he had misunderstood his vision. After all, the coyote had said, "think and look." Perhaps he was not being aggressive enough. He wandered around the immediate area, poking and investigating, but found nothing. It would help, he thought with a bit of irritation, if he had some idea what he was seeking. He returned to his fire, and realized he must have more wood for the coming night.

Owl had made several trips to his camp with armloads of sticks when he noticed a scraggly dead pine nearby. It had grown from a crevice at the back of the rock against which he camped. The tree was no taller than his shoulder. It had managed to survive in a tortuous location on the exposed face of the rock for a few years, but had now succumbed. It would be ideal fuel, Owl thought, as he broke the dried branches and piled them in the crook of his arm.

The tree had clung tightly against the rock face, and he noticed that when he pulled the twigs away, there were marks remaining on the smooth surface of the stone.

Suddenly he took a step back for a better look. The scratches just exposed had not been made by the tree, he now realized. They had been put there by a human hand. Hurriedly, in the waning light, he pulled branches and the collected debris of the years away from the rock.

There were three of the figures, human figures of varying

sizes. The largest was only half the height of a man, while the smallest was little more than a hand's span. They reminded Owl of the figures on the Story Skins far away in the lodge of White Buffalo.

He attempted to decipher meaning from these pictures. At first he thought this might represent a family unit, a warrior, his wife, and a child. Yet all three carried spears, so he decided they must be warriors with varying degrees of prestige. But why were they here?

It was almost fully dark now, and he lighted a torch to continue his examination. He also looked at the other accessible faces of the great boulder, but found no markings of any sort. He returned to the fire, though he knew there would be little sleep tonight.

He remembered White Buffalo's occasional mention of the Old Ones. There was little knowledge of these people. They had lived among the rocks and cliffs of the mountains, before the memory of tribes now in the region. Owl realized with a twinge of regret that he had been inattentive during some of the rambling lectures of the old medicine man.

He could remember only that the Old Ones had been gone for a very long time, long before the People came from the northern plains. And that migration, though recorded in the Story Skins, was before the time of his grandfather's grandfather. The strange people had left a record of their passing only in the occasional picture scratched on the surface of a rock. There were said to be many such pictures in the far recesses of the mountains, he now recalled. But why here? What was the purpose of this solitary marker, the great red stone bearing the pictures?

Crouched over his fire, deep in thought, Owl could feel the presence of the Old Ones who had made their home here. They had been people like himself, with dreams and hopes and problems of survival. Where had they come from, and why had they gone?

For some reason the first phrases of the People's death song came to him, in a comforting, enduring way:

"The grass and the sky go on forever—"

20

Although Owl could hardly wait for daylight to begin further investigation of the rock pictures, it was probably fortunate that he was forced to take time to think. Through the long time of darkness, as he tended his fire, he continued to grow closer in spirit to the long vanished Old Ones. For the first time, he began to understand them as people. Not people like himself, perhaps, not of the People, his own tribe, but still as human beings.

If, for instance, they had wintered in this area, they would have had the same needs now pressing upon him. They would have been seeking food and shelter. They would need skins for garments and for warmth, and fuel for their fires.

The Old Ones undoubtedly had enemies, too. Everyone, he supposed, had enemies, except perhaps the Hairfaces. An odd thought, he mused. He had not considered that. Did the Hairfaces have enemies in their own country,

who caused them fear? He must ask his father when he
returned to the People.

But meanwhile, he was certain the Old Ones had had
enemies. Some thought that was the reason for their disappearance. They had been killed or driven away. It made
no difference now, he had decided as White Buffalo re-
counted the legends. In fact, he had been a trifle bored by
the entire story.

Now the story had come to reality for him. He sat by a
fire, perhaps in the exact spot used many generations ago
by another young warrior. Possibly the other had been a
young medicine man, also. It seemed likely that the rock
pictures were made by a medicine man. Were they part of
a ceremony, a seeking of guidance, a search for a vision?

Owl could not decide. He was certain only that someone of the Old Ones had paused and camped here, long
enough to carve the pictures on the rock. It seemed logical that they had been seeking the same things he now required, food, shelter, protection. And probably, Owl
finally realized, they had found these necessities. It was
possible that their wintering-place might be quite near.

Their "wintering-place." *Aiee,* he was still thinking in
terms of the People. White Buffalo had told of the Old
Ones, Owl dimly recalled, as living in permanent camps,
perhaps much like the Growers. Now he was confused
again, and had no clear idea what he was looking for.

At any rate, the Old Ones had to spend the winter somewhere just as he must. Owl resumed this previous train of
thought. The place might easily be near.

By first light of dawn, he was painstakingly exploring
the area. Owl later realized that he must have passed the
opening a dozen times. He had noticed the cleft the day
before, but had assumed it to be only a shallow pocket
formed by the tumble of boulders. Two huge red stones
leaned together like gigantic lodge poles. In the doorway
thus formed had grown a thick tangle of juniper and other

brush, almost choking the opening. The impassability had been further enhanced by generations of pack rats, who had carried massive quantities of debris into the crevice.

Now he suddenly noticed that he could see a shaft of daylight beyond the tangle. He approached for a closer look, pulling dead brush, leaves, and pack rat trash from the cleft. The opening, he now became aware, was nearly tall enough for him to step through upright. And, rather than a blind end pocket in the rock, it was indeed a doorway, opening into a meadow beyond.

Astonished, Owl stepped back and looked again. From a few paces, the doorway seemed only a trash-filled crevice among many other crevices in the mountain of tumbled stone. He started to squeeze through, then paused and decided to break camp. In short order, his possessions were packed and his fire extinguished. He took one last look around the area, and a last glance at the picture-stone, now recognized as a marker for the opening of the trail. Pushing his pack and weapons ahead of him, Owl wriggled past the obstructing brush and crawled into the open on the other side.

The valley dropped away before him, ringed by sheer cliffs and rugged slopes. The floor was a mixture of grassy meadows and clumps of woodland. In the distance he could see what appeared to be a small beaver pond. Good, he nodded to himself. That meant water.

The size of the entire valley was such that one might walk around it in a day, Owl thought. He picked up his belongings and started down the slope, following what must have once been a trail. Occasionally trees blocked his path, grown large, he realized, in the intervening years since the last human foot had stepped here.

There was plentiful deer sign, both in black scars on the white bark of young aspens, and in deer droppings of various ages among the rocks. The situation looked better and better. Now if he could only find a sheltered corner that Sun Boy could look into easily, he could prepare for the onslaught of Cold Maker.

Sun Boy was well past his highest point in the south before Owl made his great discovery. He had been walking along, carefully watching in all directions. As he sat to rest, he was idly looking at the scatter of broken rocks on the ground. Suddenly, he noticed a stone which appeared to be an arrow point. Owl stepped over and picked up the fragment, turning it over in his palm. To his amazement, on the other side was a geometric design in angles of black and gray. It was not an arrow point, but a shard of broken pottery! Clay pots were not used by the People, but Owl recognized the object by his experience as a captive. He looked around, and soon found another fragment, red this time, with a wavy line across the surface. What could be the meaning? His thoughts were interrupted by the call of a jay over his head, and he glanced upward. Then he saw the lodges. There were several of them, built into the face of the cliff. Quickly he plunged into the concealment of the thicket.

For the space of many breaths, Owl lay hidden, but there was no sign that he had been seen. Cautiously, he moved so that he could peer between the leaves and evaluate the village more extensively.

After some time, it became apparent that there was no sign of life. In fact, the mud and stone lodges were, Owl now realized, in a state of advanced disrepair. Roofs had fallen in, and in some cases, entire walls had crumbled. Finally, he saw a lodge in which a large pine tree had grown up directly through the dwelling, rising the height of several men above the nonexistent roof. It must have been many years in the growing.

Finally the significance sank into his consciousness. He was looking at the homes of the long-vanished Old Ones. Curiosity urged him from his thicket, and toward the cliff. He could see a narrow path snaking its way up-ward along the face, and sought its lower end.

After several false starts, he succeeded in locating the main path, and climbed rapidly upward. He was breathing heavily by the time he stepped onto a horizontal portion of the trail, which wandered past the openings of the various dwellings. Some were little more than small caves in the rock, their ceilings blackened by the smoke of ages. Others were far more complicated lodges made of stone and mud. Owl wandered along, marveling at the structures. Some were in very fair condition, especially those protected by the overhang of the cliff face.

From the vantage point in front of the lodges, he could easily see the entire Valley of the Old Ones spread beneath him. No enemy could approach unseen. The place was completely defensible, even by only a few men. Best of all, the slanting rays of Sun Boy's torch reached under the yellow overhang of the bluff, to warm the dwellings before night. Owl realized that he had found his wintering-place.

He could not bring himself to sleep in one of the more intact lodges. The feeling of entrapment was too threatening. Finally, with darkness descending, he made a temporary camp in a sheltered corner of the sun-warmed cliff face. He could choose a more permanent shelter tomorrow.

Meanwhile, his night fire made a cheerful spot of light where none had been through endless ages since the departure of the previous inhabitants.

As he chewed his evening meal, Owl ceremoniously dropped a fragment of his precious dried meat into the fire. There was no particular need to do so. It merely seemed prudent to attempt to express gratitude to the spirits of the Old Ones.

Having appeased the spirits, he fell quickly asleep, relaxed and confident.

21

It was still dark when Owl awoke. There was a chill in the air, and the wind had changed direction. Little back-eddies stirred the coals of his dying fire, sending sparks bouncing along the ground. There was an ominous feel of expectancy. The changing wind currents moaned through empty lodges like disembodied spirits of the Old Ones.

Owl shivered and pulled his robe closer, carefully feeding small sticks into his fire. The bright glow helped his spirits somewhat. By the time he felt warm and confident again, it was becoming light. Light, that is, in tones of dull muddy gray. The sky was overcast, and Owl realized he had found his shelter none too soon.

In fact, there was much to be done before the valley became choked with snow. By full daylight he was working frantically. He had not stopped to eat. Such activity could be undertaken at leisure. Just now, every precious moment must be used in preparation. All the signs pointed to the fact that Cold Maker had initiated his first probe from the north into this region.

Rapidly, Owl selected a shelter which would suffice for the winter. Though he tried hard, he could not convince himself to use one of the lodges of the Old Ones. Several were in good condition. All he would have to do was move in. He actually went so far as to step inside one of the structures and look around. He could see that it would be ideal for his needs. The fire pit was well placed, and he could readily tell that protection from the wind was good. His mind told him that this was the place, but the old feeling of enclosure crept in. His heart refused to accept the threat of entrapment. His roots were too deep in the prairie sod. Wide spaces and far horizons were more to his desire. A twinge of homesickness for the comfortable shelter of his father's skin lodge tugged at him for a moment.

Amused at his own illogical fears, he still must find an acceptable shelter. He walked in both directions along the ledge for the distance of a bow shot, quickly examining any possibly suitable place. Finally he selected a site.

It was a small cave, near the head of the path from below. The depth was only a pace or two, merely a pocket in the soft stone. The low roof was blackened near the entrance by fires of winters gone by. A good fire would reflect heat into the hollow and provide comfort no matter how Cold Maker howled.

Owl tossed his possessions inside, and moved rapidly down the path to the trees below to gather firewood. It would take many trips up the cliff to supply enough wood for the winter. Each trip he carried as much as he was physically able, and reached the top puffing with exhaustion. At least, he told himself, this is more productive than the carrying of ore sacks.

The growing pile of firewood was stacked against the

cliff face and immediately beside his cave entrance. The branches and brush would themselves help to form a windbreak for his shelter.

The ledge directly in front of his cave was smooth and level and several paces wide. As he made each trip up and down the cliff, Owl noticed that the ledge was worn by the footsteps of the previous inhabitants. He was walking in a path worn in solid stone. How many times, he wondered, must a moccasined foot rub against the stone to produce a groove this deep? *Aiee,* every stick of wood, every twig for the fires of the whole village, must have been carried up the steep path behind him.

And what about water? The Old Ones would have used, he assumed, the clay pots. He had seen these used in such fashion. His own tribe preferred to camp near water, and then use water skins in which to carry when needed. With the problem of water in mind, Owl took time to drink long and deeply at the stream. It might be quite uncomfortable to make the climb tomorrow if the threatening storm ensued. He also resolved never to perform the upward leg of the journey without all the wood he could carry.

A band of deer flashed through the aspens and bounded across the meadow, snorting and excited over the rapid change in the weather. Owl watched them for a moment, pleased. It was good to know that meat would be available. He wondered if he could contrive a bow and arrows. That would certainly make it easier. He would try, he decided. He would probably have much time on his hands in the cold moons to come.

The wind carried moisture now. Little spatters of mist struck against his face, and the surface of the rocks beside the trail became shiny and wet. He would have to watch his footing. There were several treacherous spots on the path. He paused long enough to gather an armful of dry grass and cedar bark to use for starting his fire. This material, along with some small dead twigs, he placed carefully in the shelter of his cave before making his next trip. He must have dry tinder for a fire.

When he felt he had accumulated enough fuel for the present, Owl's attention turned from matters of necessity to those of comfort. He would prepare the best bed available. He had noticed a thick growth of juniper at the foot of the cliff, and made several trips carrying armfuls of the soft tip branches.

The path was becoming icy now, and when he almost slipped, Owl decided that now he must make do with what he had managed to acquire so far. He dumped the last armful of juniper tips into the cave, and stooped to enter. The branches he broke and trimmed into feathery fronds two or three hand spans in length. Painstakingly, he laid the branches for his bed, overlapping to cover the butt ends of each row with the soft springy tips of the next. Then he spread his elk skin over the pile and stretched luxuriously on it to rest for a moment.

The steadily dropping temperature, combined with his sudden cessation of activity, soon made him uncomfortable. He would start his fire. The rubbing sticks soon produced a glowing coal in powdery tinder, and Owl carefully blew it into flame. The cheery crackle warmed his spirits as the cave became more comfortable. He was glad to see that the wind currents allowed the smoke to draw well, moving up and out of the cave. He had worried about this. Most of his previous experience had been with movable smoke flaps on a skin lodge. How had the Old Ones been able to adjust their dwellings for changes in wind direction? He decided that in this case, the cave's inhabitants may have simply selected the best spot for the fire by trial and error. At any rate, it worked well.

What sort of a person, Owl wondered, had lighted the last fire in this cave so many winters ago? Again he felt the closeness, the kinship, with the mysterious Old Ones, as he watched the flickering pictures in light and shadow on the cave walls. He watched for a long time, deep in thought, until the fire began to die.

He stepped outside to bring more firewood, and found that the weather had changed again. It was much colder, and a still, heavy feeling hung over the valley. The wind had died, and big fluffy flakes of snow were falling. Cold Maker had arrived.

22

The snow continued through the night and all of the next day. Owl remained in his shelter, and carefully fed his fire at a slow but steady rate. He ate frugally from his store of food, slept often, and occasionally looked out to observe any changes. There were none. The snow fell softly and relentlessly, drifting slightly along the ledge. Owl ate snow as an alternative to water, but by dark on the second night in his cave he began to worry a little.

Not about water. As long as there was snow he could use that. His worry was that he would be trapped on the ledge without access to game and with his supplies dwindling. Perhaps he should move to the valley floor and try to improvise some sort of shelter.

Of course not, he reassured himself. The Old Ones had established their village here because of its practicality. They would have been unable to maintain a village of this size if it were not possible to exist here over many winters.

Still uneasy, he offered another fragment of meat to his fire
to maintain the good will of the Old Ones.

Owl understood his dilemma quite well. He was unfamiliar with the weather that might be expected here in the
mountains. His people were used to wintering along a
sheltered river course in the rolling plains. He had no idea
how cold the nights, or how deep the snow, in this valley.
Perhaps the entire valley floor would be too deep in snow
for him to move about and hunt. But no, the Old Ones had
lived here. Well, no matter now. He was here, and could
not travel with winter having arrived.

He was anxious for the snowfall to cease. When he awoke
at the following dawn Owl realized that the sky was clear,
and he rose quickly to explore the area. He wrapped himself in his rabbit cape and tied it at the waist. The spear and
one throwing stick would be his weapons.

The trail leading down the cliff proved not too bad. In
most areas the wind had prevented obstruction of the path.
One or two drifts on the downwind side of large boulders
were easily traversed. The snow was dry and powdery,
and Owl found that he could shuffle through it without
difficulty.

He kept a watchful eye for rabbits. Though he was unfamiliar with the habits of these mountain long-ears in
winter, he knew that in his own prairie country, this would
be an ideal morning to hunt.

The first rabbit eluded him entirely, bounding away at
his feet with a startling leap. He must watch more closely.

Owl spotted the next rabbit ahead of him near the path.
A clump of dry grass formed an arching protection, and
hunched comfortably beneath the concealing stems sat a
fluffy long-ear. The protective coloration was so complete
that Owl would have entirely overlooked the hiding animal except for the bright, shining eye. He began his stalk.

It was important, he reminded himself, not to look

directly into the animal's eye. That would enable the rabbit to read his thoughts. He casually continued his unaltered pace, pretending not to see his crouching prey. Then, at the right moment, without even breaking stride, Owl struck with the throwing stick. Not a throw, just a quick backhand blow, and the rabbit lay kicking in the snow. Good. This would enable him to conserve his dried provisions.

Yet another rabbit was added to his food supply in the same manner before he climbed the bluff again. The most important find of the day, however, was merely an observation.

He saw the deer herd at a distance, and noticed again how the aspens around him were marked by their chewing. The tree beside him bore black scars on the smooth white bark. He reached up and touched the highest of these marks, just above his head. Suddenly the significance sank home. He looked quickly around at other trees. He could see no marks of the animals' feeding activity that were any higher than his reach.

This gave him invaluable information. If the snow in the valley became deep, the deer would be unable to move about to any extent. They would stay in one area, and their combined trampling would pack snow firmly beneath their feet. Then, they would reach upward to chew the bark during the hardest part of the winter. And, he reasoned, if snow depth were great, they would be standing on the deeply packed substance. Then the scars on the bark would be higher than those he now observed. The marks would be visible for several years. His conclusion was very gratifying. There had been no great depth of snow in this valley for at least five or six seasons.

Owl was elated as he climbed back to his cave, carrying firewood, and with his two rabbits swinging by the hind legs. He was pleased no less by his discovery than by his use of observation and reason. White Buffalo would be proud of his pupil. He must remember to tell the medicine man when he rejoined the People.

With added confidence, Owl settled in for the winter. Each day brought, in its own way, an improvement in his condition. He improved his weapons and his garments. True, they would be objects for amusement when he rejoined his tribe, but for now they were more than adequate.

He was able to kill a fat yearling buck with his spear. By means of covering himself with his rabbit cape over his head, he found that he could move among the deer with little trouble. The technique, after all, was not much different than working among buffalo with a cape made of a calf's skin. The deer seemed merely to regard him as a strange new sort of animal, more curious than dangerous.

The food and skin of the young buck were put to good use. Owl was already planning his journey back to the People. It would begin as soon as the weather would permit. Much of the meat was dried and stored for traveling. Once he started, Owl did not want to be encumbered by stopping to hunt.

The Moon of Long Nights passed, and the Moon of Snows. At least, Owl believed them to be. He could gauge somewhat by the daily journey of Sun Boy with his torch, swinging in a low curve across the southern sky. Owl would sit at the mouth of his cave and sight across a distant mountain top, estimating the height of Sun Boy's arc at the zenith. Finally, after many days, it appeared Sun Boy was rising higher. That would signal the end of Long Nights' Moon, he believed. In a land so different from his own, it was difficult to be sure. The prediction of the deer proved accurate, and at no time were there heavy enough snows to prevent his moving about for more than a day or two.

He contrived a small waterbag from the skin of a porcupine, with hair and quills removed, and thereafter could make less frequent trips to the stream. In addition, he accidentally discovered, on a morning of melting snow, a depression in the rock near his cave. Melted snow was trickling into the basin in a steady stream. With surprise he realized that this collecting pool was intentional. The Old Ones had scraped grooves in the soft rock to channel precious drinking water into the basin for use. Thereafter, his trips to the stream were even fewer.

The Moon of Hunger followed. Owl had wondered, as a child, at the strange name for this moon. The name, he finally came to understand, had been given before the People had the advantage of the elk-dog with which to hunt buffalo. Winter had been a terrible time, a time of starvation.

Just now, however, the foremost thing in his mind about the Hunger Moon was not the Hunger Moon itself, but that which followed. Next in the order of things was the Moon of Awakening. Then the buds would begin to swell and Sun Boy would drive Cold Maker back into the mountains.

Then, Owl told himself, he could start the long journey back to his people.

23

It was in the moon that Owl believed to be the Moon of Awakening that he prepared to depart. Buds were swelling, and on the sheltered slopes where Sun Boy's torch could reach most of the day, green sprigs of grass were showing.

He had become impatient lately, each succeeding thaw giving him hope that the season was changing. Now, with all signs pointing the way, he was eager to continue his journey home.

Owl had wintered well. Long hours and days he had spent in working on and improving his few possessions. He had killed a deer during the second big snow, by standing immobile beside one of the deer paths in the woods. His spear had functioned well. He had abandoned the idea of trying to construct a bow. The available trees were not familiar to him, and he was unsure of which wood to try. Anyway, he did not appear to need a bow. His present weapons were doing nicely for his needs.

Owl glanced for the last time around the shelf that had been his home during the moons of the winter, and shouldered his pack. He had carefully extinguished his fire after making a final sacrifice of meat to the Old Ones.

Rapidly he retraced his trail of moons before, and crawled through the cleft in the rock beside the picture stone. For no good reason, he replaced brush and debris, concealing the entrance to the Valley of the Old Ones. He had grown very close in spirit to these people during the long winter. Somehow, it pleased him to think of their valley as he had found it, undisturbed, with their spirits at rest.

Turning, Owl estimated his direction of travel, and sighting on a tall peak in the distance, began a ground-covering stride. Now, he realized, was the most important time for good judgment. It would be easy for him to become so engrossed in trying to cover distance that he would forget the dangers. His longing for the open prairie and its far horizons was so strong that he found himself wanting to push on. He must remind himself continually to rest, eat, and sleep properly.

In addition, he must increasingly be on the lookout for enemies. He had moved well to the north of the Hairfaces' colony. He felt that he was also out of the country of the Mud Lodge people, but he wasn't sure. He could perhaps tell more when he reached open country.

That, of course, would bring new dangers. He must cross the territory of the Head Splitters. Although that phase might be the most dangerous of all, Owl faced it with the most confidence. The Head Splitters had customs more like his own. He understood their ways and could cope with them better than with those of the strange tribes he had met. They were, after all, buffalo people.

Additionally, if he could locate a band of Head Splitters, he might be able to steal a horse and travel better.

Owl traveled for as many days as one has fingers. Then, one morning, he topped a ridge and could see, through a pass in the mountains ahead, the plains spread before him. The grassland stretched on and on until the blue of distance blended with the blue of sky. The young man felt that he could see his homeland, and the thrill of victory kept him traveling late that night, against his better judgment.

It was still three more days before he actually left the broken foothills behind and traveled out onto the plains. It would be many days more before he found the rich deep-grass country of his people. Meanwhile, travel was faster. He must keep a close eye out for the smoke of the Head Splitters' campfires. Especially, he thought, at dawn and dusk, when the women are cooking. With this in mind, Owl spent a few minutes in a ritualistic search of the horizon twice each day. Still he had seen no sign of human life.

Almost daily, he saw bands of antelope, who watched him curiously as he passed. There were occasional small herds of buffalo. Always a few stragglers wintered in the sheltered gullies of the plains. The great herds had not yet moved from their wintering-places in the south. Owl spoke to the buffalo as he passed. The great shaggy beasts merely stood and nodded massive heads at him. Still, he began to feel that he was approaching home. He had not seen a buffalo since leaving the captivity of the Head Splitters two winters before. Now, they seemed like old friends as he spoke to them in passing.

This reminded him that it seemed like endless time since he had heard a human voice. Not since the fateful day of the escape, with the smoke-log booming and bleeding prisoners screaming. He shook his head at the -

unreality of the memory, and jogged on at a steady, ground-eating pace.

Then came the morning when he spied smoke on the horizon. It was merely a smudge at the rim of the world, far to the northeast. He studied the gray blur for a long time, and finally decided to travel straight toward it. Best to know exactly where he stood, he convinced himself. He must find if this band were really the enemy. After all, this could be a band of his own tribe, the People. The Red Rocks band sometimes came this far west, he thought.

With this sort of reasoning, Owl may have been deceiving himself a little. He was so starved for human contact that the existence of a camp, of whatever tribe, drew him like a moth to the flame. Even an enemy band were human beings.

This did not prevent caution. He estimated the camp to be more than a day's travel away, so he leisurely moved in that direction, constantly watching for any stray hunters. His caution was rewarded late that afternoon, as he spotted the stripped carcass of a buffalo at a little distance. He moved in that direction.

There was little left but the skeleton, but he could read the story easily. The skin was gone, so the animal had been butchered, not eaten by wolves and smaller predators. There were numerous hoofprints of horses, and the grass had been trampled and disturbed, verifying the presence of people.

He almost overlooked the most important sign. Protruding from under a well-cleaned shoulder blade was an arrow shaft. Owl seized it eagerly and examined its construction. The shaft had broken a hand's span in front of the feathers. Some hunter would be disappointed to lose such a well-made shaft, he knew. The stone tip was missing. It could be used again. His attention turned again to the feathering of the arrow. There were subtle differences apparent here. Even allowing for individual variation in skill and in preference, this arrow was not exactly like those of the People.

In all probability, then, the camp, less than a day's journey ahead of him, was that of a band of Head Splitters.

24

The knowledge that the camp ahead was that of the enemy made very little difference to Owl. His course was still directly toward the smoke stain on the far horizon. Now he must merely be more cautious, to avoid detection. He stayed on high ground whenever possible to improve his field of observation. Yet, he was careful not to make himself too conspicuous. When approaching the crest of each low, rolling hill, he sought the concealment of broken, rocky terrain, or the irregular lines of vegetation. His camp that night was without fire.

By late next afternoon he had moved to a jumble of boulders overlooking the distant encampment. It was a large cluster of conical skin lodges, looking much like that of his father's own band. A wave of homesickness washed over him for a moment before he reminded himself that this was the enemy. Still, these were buffalo people, men of the prairie, and he felt a strange contradictory kinship with them.

For a long time he lay on his belly and studied the camp. Judging from the number of lodges, there might be fifty or more warriors. This might even be, he realized with a start, the band of Bull's Tail, his previous captor. He was unsure how many bands there were in the Head Splitters' entire tribe. Maybe six or seven. They were constantly shifting, changing in size and strength like the bands of his own people. Political pressures, prestige, even a successful hunt or war party could attract warriors to join with an influential chief for a season.

The lodges were too far away for him to see any of the markings painted on the skins. Strange, he pondered. At a great distance, color became meaningless. One's eye could see motion or form at a much greater distance than color. He knew that many of the lodge paintings would be bright reds and yellows, but at this distance, all were hazy shades of gray-blue.

It was the same with the herd of elk-dogs, scattered in the prairie behind the camp. He could see motion and the familiar shapes, but could not identify colors of individual animals. He must get closer as darkness fell, and steal a horse to continue his journey.

Owl was so intent on the panorama before him that he committed a near-fatal mistake. He had focused his entire attention on one direction, the camp to the east of him. His usual caution had been neglected, and for the moment he had forgotten to sweep the horizon with a glance from time to time. Therefore, he overlooked the buildup of dirty-gray clouds on the horizon to the northwest. For a while, they appeared little different from the gray-blue of the distant mountains, and were easily overlooked.

By the time Owl noticed the threatening change in the weather, the storm front was rapidly developing. Cold Maker, in one last belated effort of the season, came pushing over the mountain ranges, sliding down the eastern slopes and spilling out on to the prairie. Sun Boy's torch was quickly obscured, and the changing winds carried promise of frost and snow.

Owl, trapped in the open, could do very little until darkness would hide his movements. He wrapped as warmly as he could in the assortment of skins he possessed, and waited, shivering, for nightfall. By the time of darkness, snow was falling, being driven almost horizontally by the cutting wind. Owl's feet were numb and wooden as he stumbled to his feet and started toward the camp.

He could almost believe that Cold Maker had taken a personal interest in the destruction of Owl. It was logical, his half-frozen brain told him as he plodded across the prairie. He had had the audacity to challenge Cold Maker in his own domain, and had survived. Now, the vengeful deity had waited for the proper moment, and had caught Owl off guard. The full force of the storm had been unleashed in destruction.

There was a time when he was almost ready to concede that he was beaten. He could see no way that he could possibly drag himself as far as the cluster of lodges for shelter. He was tempted to lie down and rest for a moment, to regain strength to continue. Then he remembered. This was a favorite ruse of Cold Maker, to delude his victims into a sense of security.

"Cold Maker is a liar," Coyote had once said. "He tells his victims that all will be well if they will only lie down to rest."

Those who did so, of course, never rose again, but would be found frozen after Cold Maker's departure.

Somehow, this was the focus of Owl's thoughts. His resentment of Cold Maker's treachery made his heart race and his blood pump faster. He had conquered too much treachery, he vowed, to give up now. He moved on, jogging to cover distance faster.

He must be cautious, he realized. Another of Cold Maker's tricks was to cause one to walk in a circle. Many had followed their own tracks to their death. In the darkness, this would be an easy mistake. Owl avoided this error by keeping the blast of the north wind continually on his left cheek. Eventually he would come to the camp or to the strip of timber along the creek below.

He considered for a time walking boldly into the camp and seeking shelter. He could profess friendship with Bull's Tail, one of their respected chiefs, and acquire shelter in this way. Even if they regarded him as a prisoner, there was the possibility of future escape. Persons who died under Cold Maker's onslaught had no such chance. Before he was forced to make such a decision, however, he recognized this line of thought for what it was. Anger welled up in him again at Cold Maker's treachery in confusing his brain. It was unthinkable to give one's self to the enemy. He jogged on.

Suddenly, ahead of him, out of the white wall of the driving snow, loomed darker shapes. He paused momentarily, then recognized the bending forms of trees and brush. Almost at the same time, he fell, rolling into the depression of the stream bed. Fortunately, there was no water at the point where he landed, and the clatter of gravel was obscured by the howl of the wind.

Owl sat up. The thin shelter of the strip of trees and the stream bank made the area seem like the warm inside of a lodge by comparison with the open plain. He gathered his possessions and moved among the trees, searching for the most sheltered portion of the area.

Visibility was so poor, with darkness and wind-driven snow, that he stumbled against a warm furry shape before he had any warning. There was the startled snort of a disturbed horse, and the animal moved away from him.

Aiee, what good fortune, thought Owl. He had blundered into the timber that the elk-dogs had chosen for shelter. Other dark forms moved restlessly, dimly seen among the trees. Owl shook out a length of rawhide rope from his pack. During the Moon of Long Nights he had worked on the plaiting of this device. Sooner or later, he had told himself, it would be needed. He had intended to obtain a horse when he could, and of course, one cannot steal a horse without a rope.

The animals were skittish, but he had no difficulty in slipping the rope around a neck, and the elk-dog responded to restraint. Once his hands were on it, the animal quieted. Owl ran exploring fingers over the head and neck, attempting to identify in the dark what sort of individual this might be.

The front teeth met at a good angle, telling him immediately that the horse was not too old to be of use. The ears were erect and alert. He leaned an arm across the elk-dog's withers, and it made no unusual response. He decided that this animal would satisfy his purposes.

Deftly, he tied the medicine-knot around the lower jaw, leaving the rope ends long for reins. Now he had only to wait for the storm to begin to abate. He turned the horse and leaned against the warm shoulder, on the downwind side.

Timing would be critical, he knew. If he were fortunate enough, the storm would decrease before daylight, and he could move on eastward. Several factors were worrisome to him as he stood waiting and chewing a strip of dried venison. The horse would leave tracks in the snow, but the wind might easily drift the powdery stuff and cover his trail. That would be a great joke on Cold Maker, he thought with satisfaction. It would depend much on when the storm abated and whether he was able to travel much before daylight.

Well, one thing at a time. Just now, he had beaten the storm, and had obtained the ability to travel rapidly. He rubbed his numbed fingers into the warm fur of the elk-dog, and waited.

25

Owl stood against the warm bulk of the horse and stamped his feet from time to time to keep them from growing numb. He must stay alert. Survival would depend on the decision as to when to leave shelter. Too early, he would be trapped in the open with Cold Maker still raging. Too late, he would be caught on the plain, in full view of his enemies when daylight came.

Impatiently, he waited. Finally, unable to contain himself any longer, he led the horse to the edge of the thicket and peered into the night. There were no landmarks visible in the dim white blur. Snow was still falling, but seemed less driven by the wind than previously.

An anxious thought struck him. With the wind diminishing, he would soon have no way at all to determine direction in the white expanse. Even after daylight, if the sky remained overcast, there would be loss of direction. He might easily travel in a circle, blundering back into the camp of the enemy. He would have to start on before the wind died, even at the considerable risk of freezing.

With a sigh of resignation, Owl grabbed a handful of the horse's mane and swung to the animal's back. He recognized this as a treacherous move on the part of Cold Maker to maneuver Owl into an exposed position again. He kicked the reluctant horse up out of the thicket and into the open.

The burning sting of the wind struck the left side of his face, and he wondered how he could have thought that the wind was abating. He nearly turned back to shelter, but realized he must not remain longer in the area. He turned a corner of his rabbit cape up around his face and the horse plodded ahead. Owl was careful to maintain direction of travel by keeping the force of the wind on his left. The horse continually tried to swing to the right, out of the stinging blast. Repeatedly, Owl pulled the animal's head around and enforced the action with a kick in the ribs.

It was not yet daylight when the wind died suddenly. Snow had diminished to an occasional fleck. Abruptly, Owl realized he had no idea which direction they were traveling. He could not let the horse's instinct take over. The animal would return to the Head Splitter's camp and its own kind. He stopped and dismounted, unsure of his next move. Nothing to do but wait until daylight, he supposed.

The muddy gray dawn found him standing in the middle of a flat white world. There was little to break the monotony of the snow-covered flatland, except for the marks of his horse's hooves wandering across the plain behind him. He hoped that further back the wind had covered the trail.

For a moment he considered continuing the general line of the wandering tracks, but then rejected the idea. He had no clear idea how long the horse might have attempted to change course before Owl noticed the absence of the guiding wind. He would need some sort of a sign to indicate direction.

Finally, he noticed, along the gray smudge of the horizon, a dirtier smudge. A long time he watched, as the blur became more prominent. That, he believed, would be the enemy village. The women would be building up the cooking fires as the morning routine took place. Families would be eating, and warriors would be looking after their horses in the aftermath of the storm. He devoutly hoped that the owner of this animal was a bit careless about his possessions. Perhaps the man would believe the horse had merely wandered away. Owl was certainly not equipped for pursuit or combat.

He looked at the animal actually for the first time in daylight. A clay-colored mare, sturdy in build and intelligent in appearance. She stood patiently, waiting for her rider to decide his next move. Owl liked the little mare's qualities. He only hoped that her previous owner had not regarded this as his best buffalo hunter. If she were one of his lesser animals, he would be more likely to accept the fact of her disappearance.

Anyway, he now had a mark, of sorts, to determine direction. He must put the camp of the enemy farther behind him, and at the same time head generally northeast. Eventually, in this way, he should encounter some band of the People. Or perhaps, he thought as he swung again to the back of the claybank mare, he could find a village of Growers. They often traded with everyone, and could possibly tell him of his tribe's location this season.

Sun Boy succeeded in breaking through the thick overcast at about midway through his daily arc. The thin rays from his torch gave scant comfort, but at least helped verify direction. Owl was pleased that his estimate had been nearly correct. He was traveling in a path only slightly more northerly than he had planned. He made a slight correction.

Some time later, when Sun Boy had again retreated behind the muddy gray nothingness, Owl was able to verify direction by a flock of geese. High overhead, their long wedges drew a line straight as an arrow shot across the sky. He watched and listened to their raucous clamor until they disappeared from sight and earshot, heading north.

He began to have some concern for his horse. He must, he knew, stop long enough for the animal to eat. Elk-dogs, it was known, were of a different sort than most animals. The deer, elk, and buffalo could all gorge themselves, and then retreat to methodically rechew and digest their meal at leisure. The elk-dog, however, must continually nibble. They were nearly always grazing, rather than bedding down like the other herd animals. White Buffalo would be proud that he remembered well. Just now, however, he must look for a stopping place for the night. It should furnish some degree of shelter as well as browse for the horse.

He finally saw the place, just before it became dangerously late. There was a dark gray-brown line of leafless trees and brush winding across the distant plain, marking the course of a stream. He turned the horse in that direction.

Before full dark, Owl had managed a fairly comfortable camp below the cutbank of the creek. There would be no pursuit at night in the snow, he reasoned, so he enjoyed the luxury of a fire. He stripped bark and small twigs from the cottonwoods along the stream and brought them to his carefully tethered mare. He must, at all costs, avoid the loss of the animal. The tired mare stood, eyes half-closed, contentedly chewing.

It was with a great deal of self-satisfaction that Owl finished his meager meal and took a last look along the back trail before rolling into his robes. He was all but satisfied that there was no pursuit.

The air seemed somewhat warmer. Cold Maker's medicine was weakening with the passing moons, he knew. Any storm after the start of the Moon of Awakening must be, no matter how intense, very short in duration.

And, best of all, he now possessed the means for rapid, efficient travel. In another moon, two at most, he could find his father's band and assume his position and duties as medicine man beside White Buffalo. Perhaps, he thought, he could even rejoin the People by the time of the Sun Dance in the Moon of Roses. *Aiee,* that would be a glorious reunion!

26

When Owl awoke, he discovered that Cold Maker had abandoned the goal of destroying the young medicine man. Sun Boy was just thrusting his torch over the world's rim, and a new scent was in the air, the smell of damp earth. Much of the snow was gone, melting in little rivulets. Scattered patches clung wetly, in marked contrast to the dry, powdery skiffs of the previous day. He quickly broke camp, swung to the back of the claybank mare, and started to travel. On a day such as this, one could cover much distance.

The prairie slid behind him under the feet of the little mare, and Owl exulted in the freedom of the far horizon. He had hardly realized the extent of his dread of closed places. This was country for human beings, the country of the People, where one could see to the edge of the earth. The sight was not obscured by rocks or trees, behind which an enemy could hide.

Each day the distant rolling prairie appeared slightly more green. He came to a burned area, and wondered whether the dry standing grass of last season had been fired by the medicine man of some band of the People. Perhaps only by lightning. Regardless, green sprigs were starting in profusion through the blackened stubble. Next day, he encountered buffalo, and allowed himself the luxury of a kill.

Owl tied his horse beyond a low hill, threw his elk robe over his head and shoulders, and began to approach the herd. He found that he had not lost the carefully studied skill of the buffalo medicine. He enjoyed the ability to move among the big animals, their hair now shedding in ragged patches. He recalled with amusement his resentment of his tutor for forcing him to perfect this procedure.

Owl moved among the animals perhaps even longer than was necessary, nostalgically brushing against the grazing giants. Finally he selected his quarry, and made his spear-thrust. The razor-sharp flint drove into soft flank parts, forward and up, into the region of the heart and lungs. The startled, mortally wounded cow threw up her head and ran wildly, with the other animals staring in dumb astonishment at her antics. It was not until the stricken beast lay kicking that the others began to fidget, then to pace, and eventually they ran in a clumsy, unhurried gallop over the prairie.

This became a feast of homecoming for Owl. He butchered out the choicest of cuts, all he thought he could carry. By the time he finished, a pair of buzzards were wheeling slow circles above him and waiting. He knew that at dark they would be replaced by coyotes and foxes.

Owl bundled his newly acquired food in a portion of the skin and slung it over his shoulder. Strange, he recalled. A few short moons ago, his survival had depended on the possession of a skin of poorer quality than that he was now leaving to rot. He regretted for a moment, but knew he could not take time to care for the skin. Neither could he carry it. The horse must carry food, all the meat he could conveniently pack.

That evening, Owl gorged himself shamelessly. He even rose in the night and cooked more of the savory hump meat, his first since he had been traded by the Head Splitters. That had been two, no, nearly three seasons ago.

Now, full and warm, he rolled back into his robe with a deep sense of satisfaction. He could hear the coyotes in the distance, yapping over the buffalo kill, and he was reminded that his medicine animal was still with him. He drifted into a comfortable, happy sleep.

Owl was not so confident a few suns later when he unexpectedly came across the trail of a moving group of people. From the marks of many lodge poles dragged behind elk-dogs, this was a large band. He tried to estimate the number of lodges, but could not.

The most burning question was, who were these travelers? They might easily be Head Splitters, so he must be cautious. They could just as easily be a band of the People. Their course was nearly due east, and they might be traveling toward the annual Sun Dance and Big Council with the other bands. He had no way of knowing where the Big Council might be held this season.

Ultimately, Owl decided to follow the plain trail before him. He decided that he was far enough north anyway, and could turn eastward into the main country of the People. If the band he was following proved to be one of his own tribe, so much the better. If not and they were the enemy, he could keep aware of their movements by following their trail. They would not be expecting trouble. They would not be so observant from their position of strength as would a smaller war party. He turned and leisurely followed the broad trail, observing ahead very carefully.

Owl estimated from the condition of the horse droppings that the traveling band was two or three sleeps
ahead of him. They would not be traveling nearly as rapidly as he could, so he would in time overtake them. He
was pleased at one thought. His own tracks would be
practically undetectable among the myriad he was following, in case he, in turn, were followed.

It was several sleeps before he learned for certain
the identity of the band he followed. Identification was of
a very humble type. At a night campsight of the group
ahead, he found a worn-out moccasin. It was of the distinc-
tive plains pattern, and its decorative thongs told its story
plainly. The discarded footgear was that of the People.

Probably, then, the group ahead were of the Red Rocks,
or possibly the Mountain band. Owl's heart leaped with
expectation. These were his own people ahead of him, the
People. He pushed ahead, though still with some apprehension.

After he sighted the band, his caution of the past seasons still forced him to watch them for nearly half a day
before going in. Finally, from a concealed position, he
heard the chatter of women gathering fuel for the evening
fires. Chatter in his own tongue, unheard for so long. He
rose, retrieved his horse, and walked boldly into the evening camp.

People stared at his odd garments, pointed and whispered, and dogs yapped at his heels. Owl stopped and asked
an old woman where he might find the lodge of the chief. It
was proper protocol to contact the chief immediately to pay
one's respects. In addition, the leader of this band was
probably an old friend of his father's. Owl would be welcomed as family, and he could learn news of the People.

The old woman pointed the way, and watched Owl curiously as he continued through the camp. He had not
asked which band this might be. Somehow he hated to admit his ignorance.

He led his horse among the makeshift brush and skin temporary lodges used by the People while on the move. The big lodges, made of many buffalo skins, were too cumbersome to erect at each stop. He continued in the direction indicated by the old woman, and came to a large brush shelter. Several women were busily engaged in cooking over fires in front of the shelter. Seated under the arching branches sat Black Beaver, chief of the Mountain band. He was quietly smoking.

"*Ah-koh,* my chief," greeted Owl. "I am Owl, son of Heads Off of the Elk-Dog band."

Black Beaver nodded recognition and motioned him to sit. Even though custom demanded a certain time of ritual smoking, Owl was impatient. It seemed forever before the chief offered him the pipe. He blew to the four winds, the sky and the earth, and returned the pipe ceremonially to the older man.

"Now, my son, what brings you to my lodge?" He had diplomatically refrained from comment on his guest's unorthodox appearance.

Owl longed to blurt out his entire story, but held himself in check. It would not be seemly. He would begin by asking the chief's hospitality.

"I would ask the shelter of your lodge, my chief," he began. "I have traveled far."

Black Beaver's eyes opened wide. To Owl's surprise, the chief appeared to nearly lose his composure.

"Of course," he finally nodded. "I only thought you might wish to stay with your wife and her people."

"My *wife*?" Owl's head swam. He completely failed to comprehend.

"You did not know?" Black Beaver was astonished in his turn. "I thought it your reason for being here!"

"But I have no wife," the confused Owl blurted. Then, slowly, a long-forgotten thought stirred. The Mountain band of the People. Had that not been Willow's? Could it be? But, he had seen her clubbed to the ground. Could the girl have survived, and lived to escape?

"Willow?" he breathed at last. "Willow is *here*?"

"Of course, my son. Your daughter, too. They do not know you are here?" The chief motioned to a young woman, who slipped quietly away among the brush shelters.

Owl was standing, dumbfounded. "Daughter?"

"Of course! Wait—you know nothing of this? Then Willow—she still thinks you dead!" Black Beaver became as excited as Owl had ever seen a man in his position.

There was a sudden rush from behind, and Owl was nearly bowled over in a flurry of feminine affection. Now the chief's composure was completely broken. He chuckled.

Willow straightened and spoke.

"Forgive me, my chief," she began.

Black Beaver waved a hand in dismissal.

"Go now," he smiled. "You have much to tell each other." He spoke again to Owl. "Come back when you have visited with your family. We will talk again."

27

The next few days were a confusion of ecstasy for Owl. So many new ideas and experiences were thrust upon him that he thought his head must burst. Willow's family welcomed him as a long lost son. They could hardly wait to provide him with buckskins and moccasins, and to invite friends to visit and meet their new son-in-law.

Owl made the adjustments slowly, only gradually realizing the prestige that he had brought to the girl's parents. *Aiee,* to have a son in the family who was a medicine man of the People, who had traveled far and seen many things! One who had bested the Head Splitters, and even the unknown hair-faced tribe far to the southwest. His medicine must indeed be strong.

Willow's father, White Hawk, was a tall warrior of middle age, athletic yet a quiet thinker. His pride was expressed in conversation with the younger man. He asked intelligent questions about the far tribes and their

ways. Owl related well to him immediately. In some ways
he reminded the young man of his own grandfather, the
Coyote.

Even more striking was the resemblance of his mother-
in-law to his own mother, the Tall One. He was not surprised to learn that her name was Tall Grass, and that she
had in fact been called the "Tall One" as a child. It was
easy to see where Willow had inherited the pride and
spirit that he had so admired.

The other member of the family was a younger brother,
called Chipmunk by the band. He had not yet received warrior status. This reminded Owl with some chagrin that he
himself had no name of adult status. Eventually, he would
accede to the title of White Buffalo, but for the present he
still had only his childhood name. At least, he thought to
himself, somewhere along the path he had lost the designa-
tion "Little" Owl. No one seemed to notice his dissatisfac-
tion with his name, so he said nothing.

Chipmunk followed Owl with adoration. He received
much status among his peers as the brother-in-law of the
great medicine man who had now married into the band.
At times the boy became a real nuisance, especially when
Owl and his wife tried to be alone. Tall Grass finally intervened, and the situation improved somewhat.

One very difficult step for Owl was to think of himself
as a father and head of a family. The small girl with the
big dark eyes of her mother was slow at first in accepting
him, but soon would curl against his chest in sleep, and
chatter happily to him at play. She was called Red Bird,
after the bright scarlet bird of the thick bushy canyons.
Owl loved to watch the child. Her bright eyes and graceful movements, even as a child of but one summer, reminded him of her mother.

And Willow! *Aiee,* it was as if they had been separated
forever when they were reunited. In other ways, it seemed
they had never been apart. They made love whenever they

could, and the understanding people of the band respected their privacy.

They had much to talk about and share. Many times both would start to speak at the same time, then they would laugh together and try again.

"You first."

"No, you, my husband."

Gradually, they learned each other's stories. Each had been told that the other was dead. Apparently their captors had used this as a device to prevent their collaborating in another escape attempt.

Willow was reluctant to tell her story, preferring to ask about Owl's experiences. Finally, in the privacy of a sunny hillside one afternoon, he insisted on hearing the entire tale.

"How did you escape? What about Many Wives?"

"Many Wives is dead. I killed him." Her eyes studied the grass beside them. Owl could see that this was as painful a memory for the girl as those that scarred his own past. He took her in his arms.

"I will tell you, my husband. Then we will speak no more of it."

Willow had half-wakened after the blow of the club, to find her hair and face sticky with clotted blood. Her head throbbed beyond belief, and she had no strength to move. Through the dim haze of her pain came the constant thought that Owl was dead, or worse. She sobbed quietly.

While she lay in this stuporous state, one of the riders returned for a last look and discovered that she still breathed. He shouted to Many Wives, and the entire group returned. She later could vaguely recall being thrown across the back of one of the horses, and of the blinding pain which drove through her injured head. Again she sank into unconsciousness.

The next few days were a blur of agony, as her head pounded whenever she moved. The other wives tried to help her to clean her bloodied face and hair, and to help her eat.

Meanwhile the sadistic Many Wives seemed to become almost crazed by the turn of events. The thought that a woman who was his property had been possessed by another man was totally unacceptable to him. He would shriek and rant at her, and his sexual demands became intolerable. Even before she was able to be up and about, he would demand frequent submission. His demands were sadistic, painful, and degrading.

Sometimes, after a cruel session in the robes, Many Wives would taunt her by threatening to "throw her away" to the warrior society. Willow was aware of this custom among these people. An unfaithful wife could be given by the husband to the men of the tribe, to be repeatedly raped by any and all. It was, in effect, a death sentence.

"You want other men?" he taunted. "You will wish you could return to the arms of Many Wives!"

Despite these frequent threats, he made no move to carry out such an action. Apparently his pride would not allow him to give up such a possession as a beautiful enemy captive. The girl kept hoping that his sadistic ardor would cool, but instead it became worse and more painful with each dreaded episode. She must take action if she were to survive. She might be killed in the attempt, but that was better than the continued degradation.

Her decisive move came after a session in the robes. She had attempted to comply with what she knew were his desires. She struggled just enough to provide the resistance she knew he enjoyed, to achieve satisfaction for him. Then, after he had rolled aside and lay sleeping off the effects of his activity, she cautiously drew out the small flint knife she had been concealing.

The slash across the throat was not quite from ear to ear. Many Wives woke with a scream which never reached his lips. The girl was able to watch the terror in his eyes as he choked, realized that he was drowning in his own blood and fought for his life's breath. Somehow, there was less satisfaction than she had expected.

The other women looked on, horrified, but there was no outcry. Willow calmly turned, lifted the lodge lining, and crawled under the outer skin into the night. Then, thinking more clearly, she returned to gather some food and small articles of clothing.

The dumbfounded girls still sat stunned, but one told her in brief sign talk that they would raise no alarm until she was gone. Some of the others appeared to be also preparing to flee as Willow slipped again to freedom.

She untied the best of Many Wives' buffalo runners from behind the lodge, and slowly led the horse toward the stream. This attracted no attention. She would appear to be merely one of the wives caring for her husband's favorite elk-dog.

Safely beyond the stream and screened by the trees, Willow kicked the animal into a lope. She hoped the other girls could make their escape also, but felt that they were on their own, as she was. Their best defense was to scatter, like quail in the fall grasses.

Distance fell behind her, and by first gray light of dawn she was sure there was no pursuit. She had succeeded.

28

Owl held the girl in his arms and the two rocked softly, tenderly sharing the moment.

"So, I traveled until I reached the People."

"When did you learn you were pregnant?"

"I already knew that, Owl. That was one reason I had to escape. I could not bear your baby among the Head Splitters. The child of our love must be raised by the People."

He chuckled and hugged her more closely.

"Child of my life's springtime," he teased, "it makes no difference at all, but you know the chances are very poor that the baby is mine. You were with Many Wives so long, and we were together only one night."

Tears came to her eyes, and for a moment she pushed him away in anger. Then her face softened and she cuddled against him again.

"Of course," she said gently, "you did not know. Many Wives was unable to father a child. That is why he tried with every young woman he could buy. Owl, you are the only man who could be the father of Red Bird." She looked directly, lovingly into his eyes. "Did you not see how much she looks like you?"

Yes, Owl thought, the child did resemble him a great deal. He had merely assumed that they would never know the exact truth. He had come to love the child as his own, and was prepared to raise her with that presumption, but this was even better. *Aiee*, this was indeed good medicine! The child was the proof of their one ecstatic night together. He clasped Willow closely to him.

Owl could almost feel sympathy for the strange, troubled Many Wives. The Head Splitter chief, though wealthy, had been tragically unhappy. His death, far from a brave death with dignity, had been an ignoble end. Both tribes would talk of this event about the fires for many seasons.

Aiee, Owl thought. What a way to meet one's end! He could imagine the horror of waking to strangle in one's own blood. Many Wives would have lived long enough to understand what was happening and realize that he had been bested by this slim girl of the enemy. The hair prickled on the back of Owl's neck at the thought. He could hardly grasp the idea that this soft female creature curled against him could be capable of such an act. Still, he was tremendously proud of her. How fortunate he was to have such a woman call him "husband."

How fortunate he was anyway, he realized. Aside from the fact that Willow's spirit and example had undoubtedly kept him alive, there was every indication that his medicine was strong. His good fortune had been too great to be mere accident. And, now that he was ready to accede to the full duties of the medicine man, he must begin work on his medicine.

Willow was delighted to help him. He began to gather and dry various plants which he noticed in their travel. With Red Bird safely in the care of her doting grandparents, Owl and his wife would travel parallel to the moving band, investigating every nook and meadow for useful herbs. He freely instructed Willow in their identification and use. The wife of a medicine man was hardly less important than he.

The Mountain band was traveling toward the Big Council, as he had guessed. It would be held this season on the river the People called Oak River. There were bluffs and low flatlands in that area, and his father-in-law assured him that it would be a good place to cut poles for the lodge of the young couple. Cottonwoods grew in the flats in thick profusion, tall, slender, and straight. The women were already preparing skins and sewing the lodge cover for their home.

Meanwhile, they continued to stay in the lodge of White Hawk. This was customary, to live with the parents of the wife until one's own lodge was ready. Then, it became optional, in a case such as this, which band they would join. Owl was afraid this might present a problem, but found that Willow had already decided.

"Of course we will join your people. You are the medicine man of the Elk-dog band."

He was glad that she understood. His debt to White Buffalo was one that he could never repay. It was his duty to the band of the old man to carry on his work.

The days passed pleasantly in travel. Owl found time to talk ceremonially with Black Beaver from time to time. They talked of tribal politics, and mutual acquaintances. Yes, Owl's family was well, the chief told him. His father was well respected by the entire tribe. The People had become a powerful force on the plains because of the power of Heads Off and his elk-dog medicine.

Owl had heard this saying all his life. He had been bored with it as a child. Now, from a more mature viewpoint, he began to appreciate the significance of the story. He longed to sit with his father for man-to-man talk. He would tell him of his experiences with the Hairfaces, and let his father know that Owl understood why he had left them.

He longed, too, for the coming chance to tell White Buffalo of all the wondrous medicine he had observed. He doubted that he could adequately describe the smoke-log, and the carts pulled by spotted buffalo. Perhaps the old medicine man could tell him more of the use of the yellow medicine stones.

He had tried to tell Willow of these things. She had been fascinated by his descriptions of the strange multicolored birds raised by the Hairfaces. They were like turkeys but smaller, and could be killed and eaten when the Hairfaces wished, just as if they were dogs. Owl thought perhaps she believed this an exaggeration. She preferred to hear about El Gato's final flight off the mountain. He did not even tell her about the prisoner staked to the wall in the medicine lodge.

In one other area he must not share his secrets with anyone, however. He was assembling his medicine pouch. The contents must always be secret. Even if seen, they would be meaningless to anyone else but would represent the best and strongest of his own medicine.

At his request, Willow constructed a small pouch of soft buckskin. Without his asking, she and her mother decorated the bag with quills in a traditional design of the People, representing the owl. He was pleased with the result. From this time forth, the medicine pouch must be with him always. No one must ever open it, or know its contents except himself. He began to gather the medicine things.

There was a small piece of buckskin from the breech clout he had worn at the time of his escape. *Aiee,* that would be powerful! He added a splinter of the flint from which he had made weapons, and a tuft of hair from his elk-skin robe. Rabbit fur, plucked from the edge of his cape, and a fluffy feather he had picked up and saved from the owl which had helped him with the rabbit hunt. There was a triangle of red pottery from the Valley of the Old Ones. This should be ancient medicine, and very strong.

A few blades of grass from the site of his buffalo kill were wrapped carefully around a tuft of the animal's wool. A knot plaited of hairs from the tail of his claybank mare acknowledged the medicine that helped him survive the storm and evade the Head Splitters.

One more item found its way into the pouch. It was a wisp of shiny black hair. He had stealthily cut this talisman from the very tip of Willow's long tresses one morning as she lay sleeping beside him. This, he considered, might well be the most important of all his medicine.

29

The site on Oak River that had been chosen for the Sun Dance was one of Owl's favorites. Each year a location was selected for the next year's meeting, and some were favorable enough that they would be chosen again in a few seasons. The Oak River site was one of these. Owl could remember at least two other councils held here during his childhood.

A bend in the river, shaped like a fully drawn bow, enclosed a level area of meadow large enough for the hundreds of lodges of the People. Families in each band would still be within the river's arc, and not too far from water. The People enjoyed swimming, and the clear stream would be filled with splashing children for most of the time of the council.

An area upstream was designated for drinking water and for filling waterskins for cooking. Elk-dogs were to be watered downstream, below the swimmers. There was sometimes encroachment, but no big problems usually arose. The use of the respective areas was enforced by the warrior societies, and in the case of the area for cooking and drinking, by the shrill resentment of the women. There were few violations.

It was late in the Moon of Roses when Black Beaver led his Mountain band into the council site. Young men had ridden ahead from a day's journey out. There were friends and relatives to greet, and tales to tell of the year's activities. Some people already at the camp rode out to meet the newcomers, and a festival atmosphere prevailed amid talk and laughter and warm greetings.

The self-appointed messengers had returned with the news that only two other bands were already at the camp ground. No, Owl's Elk-dog band was not one of them.

Finally, too impatient to wait, Owl rode ahead with White Hawk to see the encampment. They stopped on the rim of the bluff overlooking the river, and gazed across at the mushrooming village. The buzz of camp life drifted across the valley to their ears, and the old excitement of the occasion began to stir Owl's blood. Dogs yapped excitedly.

Each band was assigned a specific area in the camp circle, corresponding to their chiefs' places in the council. Owl could see that the Northern band was here, and already well settled. That was as it should be. Their chief, old Many Robes, was also the real-chief of all the People. It was the responsibility of his family to prepare the Dance Lodge. The large structure of poles and brush was already well under construction in the center of the camp. There were men on top of the lodge, and others were handing up armfuls of brush to be tied in place.

Another motion caught the corner of his eye, and Owl shifted his gaze. A lodge skin was being lifted into place by a group to the southwest of the Dance Lodge. That would be the Red Rocks band. Apparently they had only recently arrived, for a number of their lodges were still merely pole skeletons, with the lodge covers laid out flat on the ground ready to hoist into position.

The spaces assigned the other bands were still empty. Owl mentally noted the area between the two already present, and to the northwest of the Dance Lodge. That would be the camping site of the Mountain band. Directly on the south side of the circle would be his father's Elk-dog group, formerly called the Southern band. To the northeast would be the Eastern band. The area to the southeast was left open as a doorway, just as a lodge's doorway faces southeast.

The two men decided to ride on down and pay their respects to the real-chief. They threaded their way down the bluff and splashed across the gravel bar at the crossing. Confusion was everywhere. Children chattered at play, dogs barked, women laughed and called to each other at their daily tasks.

Somewhere somebody was cooking hump ribs, and the smell nearly drove Owl to distraction. He felt that he had never had enough meat to eat since his reunion with the People. His tremendous appetite for broiled hump ribs had become a family joke.

A man lounged against a willow back rest outside his lodge and smoked thoughtfully. He nodded and smiled as they passed.

They located the chief's lodge with no difficulty, and dismounted to pay their respects. Old Many Robes had changed little, as far as Owl could see. He had always seemed incredibly old to the boy. His mind still appeared as sharp as the snap of a fox's teeth, however. He remembered Owl, and stated that he was delighted to hear that rumors of Owl's death were unfounded.

They smoked and then prepared to depart, just as the first of the Mountain band came over the bluff's rim and started the steep descent to the river. They hurried to assist in the preparation of the lodge site. Tall Grass paced off the circle for the lodge, and then tied three of the poles together to form the initial tripod.

"Now," she instructed, "you men go and cut poles for the lodge of Owl and Willow. We can do this."

It was a wise suggestion; with hundreds of families moving into the area, new lodge poles would become scarce. In addition, the good camp sites would all be taken.

They took a horse to drag their poles, and spent until nearly dark cutting and trimming the best cottonwood poles they could find. When they returned, Tall Grass had laid out the circle for the new lodge.

"The cover will not be ready for a while," she admitted, "but we will set the poles. This will save a good spot for your lodge."

Owl realized that his mother-in-law wished to keep her daughter nearby as long as possible.

The men helped to lift the heavy lodge skin into place, and soon White Hawk's lodge was established in the new camp. Owl could still barely comprehend that the skeleton of new-cut poles in the adjacent spot would soon be the lodge of his, Owl's own family.

Two suns later, the Eastern band arrived. Again, there was much laughter and renewal of old friendships and acquaintances, much visiting of relatives, and increased quantities of confusion and barking of dogs. An incident also occurred which to Owl marked his first venture into full-fledged duties as a medicine man.

As the lodges of the newly arrived group were tilting into position, an anxious young woman came looking for him. Their Eastern band, she told Owl, had no medicine man, and her child was very ill. Owl had been pointed out as one who might help.

Owl was reluctant at first. He told the woman of his recent return from captivity. He had had no time to construct a headdress or rattles, and had no drum, even. Then he saw tears in the eyes of the young mother, and agreed to try.

He called to Willow, and asked her to borrow a drum. She darted away among the lodges. Then he rummaged in their possessions and brought out some of the herbs and grasses he had been collecting. He would wear his rabbit cape, for want of anything more suitable. He did take the time to paint his face, with a broad red band beneath each eye, across the cheekbone, and a narrow stripe of yellow down the nose.

Willow returned with a small drum, her eyes shining with excitement. They followed the young woman back to her lodge, stooped, and entered.

As their eyes adjusted to the dim light, Owl saw a boy of perhaps six summers lying on a robe. His eyes were wide open, and a look of fear and anxiety was fixed firmly on his face.

"He cannot stand or even sit," the mother was saying. "He falls over."

Owl nodded, and spoke a greeting to the husband, who hovered anxiously over the bed of his son. To himself he wondered, what manner of evil is this? He had expected merely the fever, or perhaps evils of the stomach. This was completely outside his experience. Well, first things must come first.

He took a pinch of plant material from a pouch and tossed it into the fire. A puff of fragrant smoke arose, and he nodded to Willow, giving her the necessary rhythm for the drum. The soft beat began, and Owl stepped into the cadences of the dance. The words of the chant came slowly. It had been long since he had practiced, but at last he finished the song, threw another pinch of incense at the coals, and turned to examine the child.

To his surprise, the skin was not flushed with fever. Slightly warm, perhaps, but not burning. The large dark eyes followed him, as he ran his hands over the boy's arms and legs. Again he encountered a surprising thing. The child's extremities were completely limp. Owl was

reminded of a deer he had once seen with a broken neck.
The animal had been completely alert but unable to
move. Yet in this case there was no injury. Could there be
something else about the neck?

Owl ran gentle fingers up the sides of the boy's throat
and moved the head quietly. He felt the scalp itself,
searching over the surface for some hint. Then something
touched his finger tip, something cool and smooth and
round, behind the left ear. He parted the hair gently and
felt more closely. Yes, it was there.

A fat, blood-swollen tick was attached firmly to the
skin in the hollow behind the ear. The creature was as
large as the ball of his thumb. Could this be the cause of
the illness? Owl wasn't sure, but it was certainly evil-
looking enough. He would assume that it might be, and
act accordingly. He thought it best, however, to conceal
his find in case it was not the problem.

White Buffalo had coached him carefully in sleight-of-
hand, and made him practice long. With an exclamation,
Owl jumped and threw his head aside, drawing the attention of the observers from the child. At the same time, he
deftly plucked the insect free with a quick jerk and palmed
the creature.

Standing, he nodded to Willow for a drumbeat, and
started a triumphal dance around the fire. In a moment he
tossed another pinch of medicine, and with it the offend-
ing bloodsucker, completely unnoticed.

At the end of the dance, he gave the mother a sprig of
herb, to be crushed and given in water to the child. He
would, he told them, return the following evening.

On the way back to the lodge, Owl was very dissatis-
fied. He had no idea whether the tick had been the cause
of the problem. Suppose the evil spirit was still within the
child? Of one thing he was certain. White Buffalo had always reminded him: In a day, an illness will be either better or worse. He slept poorly that night.

As it happened, the child was remarkably better. Before the appointed time even, the boy's father appeared, recounting in awed phrases how the youngster was able to sit up, eat, and even stand. Owl quickly rose to go and see, and Willow accompanied him.

The boy did indeed look almost well. Owl attempted to look as if he had known it all along, and Willow gazed at him with such adoration that he was embarrassed. The delighted parents insisted on presenting Owl with a beautifully tanned otter skin.

He still had his doubts, but tried not to show his insecurity. By evening, his reputation as a skilled medicine man was known throughout the camp.

30

It was still several suns before the Elk-dog band approached the site of the Sun Dance. Scouts reported the column to be two sleeps away. Immediately Owl began to fidget. He became moody and irritable. Even little Red Bird failed to break through his preoccupation. Finally, on the advice of her mother, Willow drew him aside.

"My husband," she began, "go to meet your family. Red Bird and I will stay here, and I will be working on our lodge." Here she snuggled against him seductively. "You would be away from us only one sleep."

Owl protested, but could see the wisdom of the plan. His parents deserved an opportunity to become accustomed gradually to all the changes before them. He could have a little time to inform them of his marriage and his daughter before the shock of meeting their new relatives. And *aiee*, he had almost forgotten. They still thought him dead!

Much as he would miss Willow, he finally consented to start next morning because the plan was good. He would probably save her much embarrassment by giving his parents advance notice.

The claybank mare moved well, and Owl thoroughly enjoyed the trip. He stopped to rest when Sun Boy's torch was high. He drank from a cold spring which came out of a hole in the hillside, and chewed some of the pemmican his wife had sent with him. The mare grazed along the hillside until Owl swung up again to proceed.

The shadows were growing long when he sighted the night camp of his father's band. Owl came near the closest of the flimsy brush shelters, and dismounted to walk on. An old woman was gathering fuel along the grassy hillside. She glanced up, then suddenly screamed and threw her armful of buffalo chips in the air.

"Aiee!" she screeched. "It is the ghost of Owl!"

Turning, she fled toward the camp, still shouting unintelligibly. People came running, accompanied by the inevitable barking dogs.

Somehow, Owl had not realized the impact that his return would create. His progress through the camp was impeded for a time by the crowd of curious people. Young men who were his contemporaries pushed forward to clasp his hand and welcome him home. They were more mature, heavier, than he remembered them. He realized that he himself had changed.

His brother Eagle shouldered through the crowd, still appearing healthy and athletic. Eagle fell in beside Owl and the two walked on toward their parents' brush lodge.

"It is good to see you, my brother," Eagle began. "You have grown up!"

"You have, too! Have you a wife?"

"Yes, and a small son."

"I have also, but mine is a daughter."

The two laughed and continued on their way.

Their mother looked up from her cooking, recognized the son she thought lost, and stood speechless for a moment. Then she gave a shriek of joy and ran to meet him. Heads Off emerged from the shelter and came quickly after her.

The curious crowd began to melt away in deference to the privacy of the reunion. For a time it seemed that everyone must talk at once.

"*Aiee,* my small brother has a wife and child!" announced Eagle proudly.

"Is this true, my son?" His mother appeared concerned.

"Yes, Mother. I am sure you will love her as I do. Her name is Willow."

"Is she of the People?" asked his father.

"Yes, the Mountain band. I met her while we were prisoners of the Head Splitters."

"*Aiee,* we thought you dead!" Tall One was still not accustomed to his return. "The men found your camp, and blood on a stone."

"It was not my blood, Mother. I broke a man's face with the stone before I was captured."

How much more to the story than that, Owl thought. It will take long to tell.

For a long time the family sat and listened to his account. Owl's grandparents, Coyote and Big-Footed Woman, joined the circle. Eagle brought his wife, a handsome girl Owl did not remember from their childhood, and proudly introduced her and a fat baby. Owl exclaimed appropriately. His brother, a family man!

Just as amazing to him was his younger sister, Dove Woman. She had been a child when he left, and was now a strikingly beautiful woman. Her gaze of adoring wonder for the brother now restored to her family was almost an embarrassment to him.

After the initial dialogue, as things became a bit quieter, Owl found opportunity to speak to his father alone.

"Father, I found a tribe of your people," he began haltingly. "I was their prisoner."

Owl thought he had never seen such a look of love and compassion on his father's face. The older man understood full well the implications of the simple statement. He knew the sort of treatment which would have been accorded a half-breed prisoner.

"I am sorry, my son." He reached a hand and gave a firm fatherly squeeze to Owl's shoulder. A shoulder, Owl thought, marked with the ugly purple welts of the cat.

"I can now understand, Father, why you left your tribe to become one of the People."

The eyes of Heads Off became misty with tears as he recalled how hard he had tried to return to his own. Why had he ever wanted to? It was difficult to remember that he had once been Juan Garcia, only son of the wealthy Don Pedro Garcia. These, the People, were his people.

"It was bad, my son?"

Owl nodded, noticing for the first time that his father was a little older, a little grayer around the temples. And the facial hair, he now realized, was sprinkled with frost.

"Yes, but I am back now with the People." He went on quickly, "I have seen many wondrous things, and I will tell you of them all. But now, I must go and see White Buffalo. I am ready to join him as a medicine man!"

It was a moment before Owl realized that everyone was staring at him sadly. Shocked tragedy was reflected in their faces. Something was badly amiss.

"What is it?"

"Owl," his mother finally spoke, "White Buffalo is dead, since the Moon of Snows."

"Then, I must see Crow Woman," Owl rose to leave, "and I will be needed as medicine man."

"No." His father motioned him to sit again. "She is dead, too. Crow Woman seemed lost without her husband, and she soon gave up."

There was an awkward silence. Owl sensed that there was more to the story. Everyone appeared acutely uncomfortable. Finally, his father spoke again.

"Two Dogs is medicine man. He has taken over the medicine of White Buffalo."

31

Two Dogs! Owl's childhood enemy, the perennial bully, had originally been one of his main reasons for entering the medicine man's apprenticeship.

"But, how?" Owl stammered. "How could he be a medicine man?"

The story was quickly told. After the loss of Owl, old White Buffalo had become very depressed. He now had no possibility at all for an understudy to learn his buffalo medicine. He had begun to age rapidly, appearing not to care what happened.

Into this situation had stepped Two Dogs. He was still a bully, and as he matured, his added physical ability had made him even more sadistic. White Buffalo, in spite of his applicant's complete lack of proper motivation, had accepted him in desperation. Time was running out.

From the beginning, Two Dogs assumed an arrogant, superior attitude. Far from the humble apprentice, he soon bullied the old man unmercifully. It became obvious that White Buffalo had no control over the situation whatever. The Elk-dog band saw, but no one seemed to know how to proceed. Crow Woman cried quietly most of the time.

Two Dogs rapidly assumed the use of the medicine man's equipment, even wearing some of his robes and ornaments. Soon White Buffalo had lost all initiative to resist.

There were those, it is true, who insisted that Two Dogs was possessed of powerful medicine. How else could it be that he grew stronger while White Buffalo became weaker? After all, the band was in need of a medicine man, and here was a strong replacement for the now senile old man. While the band argued, privately of course, Two Dogs became more arrogant, and White Buffalo became more ineffectual. When the weakening medicine man finally died in his sleep, there were even some who whispered that Two Dogs' medicine had killed him.

There was no way, of course, to prove this theory. Already Two Dogs had gone to the medicine man's lodge and appropriated all of the accoutrements of the office. He made a public ceremony of burning the old man's medicine pouch. He donned the sacred white cape and performed the Dance of the Buffalo, while one of his friends tapped the cadence on the medicine drum. Crow Woman watched and cried silently.

At the end of the dance, Two Dogs announced that henceforth he would be known as White Buffalo. The crowd melted away, troubled but unsure. Who could challenge the authority of the medicine man?

It became inadvisable to criticize the new medicine man. Two of his friends had now become his assistants, and their ears were everywhere. A woman spoke out in a semipublic place, that Two Dogs had corrupted the authority of the office. One of his assistants was then seen to be listening. For the next two suns the woman writhed in abdominal pain, retching constantly. The People became more apprehensive about disagreement with the new medicine man.

Still, no one called him White Buffalo, except to his face.

"He is a poor medicine man, Owl," stated Coyote, and the others nodded. "He thinks only of his own power, and he has not studied his lessons well. He fired the grass at the wrong time this season, and we had to move to find buffalo!"

Owl saw little that could be done. The man was a charlatan, but he possessed the symbolic white cape and other symbols of authority. It would be difficult to challenge such medicine.

Some of Two Dogs' medicine, like the induction of vomiting in the woman who challenged his authority, was simple. It would require only a pinch of certain herbs, secretly introduced into her food, Owl knew. But there was no real cause for challenge. The wrong time for burning was understandable. Anyone could make such an error in judgment, he realized.

"I will go and pay my respects to him," Owl finally decided. Over the misgivings of the others, he rose and threaded his way to the shelter pointed out as that of the medicine man.

Two Dogs was seated in a presumptuous shelter, surrounded by a disgusting array of fine skins and other medicine items. Owl was about to greet him, when his way was suddenly barred by another man wearing the headband of a medicine man's apprentice.

Owl recognized the sneering face as that of one of Two Dogs' childhood friends. The other showed no sign of recognition.

"I would speak with the medicine man," Owl began.

The man said nothing. "You remember me! I am Owl. We grew up together. I, too, am a medicine man." There was still no answer.

"Who is here?" asked Two Dogs haughtily, though he could plainly see all in the firelight, as well as hear the conversation.

"He says he is a medicine man," stated the apprentice with a chuckle.

Two Dogs waved his arm in dismissal.

"Tell him to go away. He is an impostor. I am medicine man to the Elk-dog band."

He made another sweeping gesture, and a puff of smoke rose from the fire. A revolting display of dramatics, thought Owl.

"White Buffalo says you are to leave," the apprentice was saying.

"I heard." Owl turned to depart.

Things were indeed difficult. There was no precedent for this sort of situation. Normally, disputes could be settled by the council, and enforced by the warrior society. In this case, however, the chief presiding over the Elk-dogs' council was the father of one of the parties involved. The other chiefs of the band would be reluctant to take sides. To side with Heads Off and his family would provoke the wrath of the medicine man, who already had a reputation as a dangerous man.

On the other hand, there was no wish to abandon Heads Off, one of the most admired chiefs of all the People.

Owl was thinking of these things as he returned to his parents' fire.

"He would not talk to me."

There was no surprise in the faces of the others.

"Coyote," Heads Off was speaking, "what is the custom in a thing of this sort?"

Coyote had spent many days attempting to answer this same question. He could not remember such a problem in his lifetime. *Aiee,* if he could talk to White Buffalo for a little while. But, that, of course, was the problem. White Buffalo was gone.

It would be very simple, he thought, if some mishap would occur to Two Dogs. It was tempting, but no, it would not do. Among the foremost taboos of the People was murder. Besides, even if it could be accomplished, suspicion would fall on the family of Heads Off.

Even, he reminded himself, if someone else were actually guilty. Certainly, there were many who would wish Two Dogs dead. He hoped no one would feel obliged to take action. He spread his hands in frustration at his son-in-law's question.

"There is no custom, Heads Off. It has never happened before. The Elk-dogs' council might decide, except that it involves the family of the chief."

A sudden thought occurred to him. The band would reach the camp of the Sun Dance tomorrow.

"*Aiee,* of course!" he exclaimed. "Why did I not think of this? You can request a decision from the Big Council at the first meeting three suns from now!"

32

Many Robes of the Northern band had been real-chief of all the People for many seasons. His tenure had seen and survived many threats and many changes. There had been the constant skirmishes with the Head Splitters, and the usual political stresses of his position. He had even weathered the cultural shock of the advent of the elk-dog. That change had been far-reaching.

The change in hunting methods and in warfare had converted the People from a defensive, timid tribe. Now they were a respected power on the plains, one even the mighty Head Splitters would hesitate to challenge.

But now came an internal crisis among the People that threatened to tear the tribe apart. Many Robes knew the danger was real. Long ago a tribe to the north had split in two over a minor disagreement between two chiefs. No longer strong enough to withstand pressure from their enemies, one group had been exterminated. The other had lost prestige and size, and was even now threatened with extinction by the surrounding tribes. This, Many Robes was firmly convinced, must not happen to the People.

But how to avoid it? *Aiee,* people were angry! There were those loyal to each of the two medicine men of the Elk-dog band. Each group claimed that their own possessed the true medicine of old White Buffalo, and that the other was an impostor. White Buffalo had been one of the greatest of medicine men. Many Robes had admired the diplomatic manner in which the old man had adjusted. The threat to his medicine with the coming of the strange hair-faced Heads Off had been great. The medicine man had been able to adapt, allowing the new medicine of the elk-dog to work with his buffalo medicine to the good of all.

But now, the powerful white cape was in the possession of Two Dogs. This young man had had a poor reputation, it seemed. His decision to make something of his life had been welcomed by his band. How could anyone have known that he would abuse the authority? Or, for that matter, that Owl, son of Heads Off, would return after being given up for dead?

Heads Off had avoided a confrontation within the band by calling for a decision in the Big Council. A wise move, Many Robes realized. However, it certainly made the job of the real-chief more difficult. There was a space of less than two suns after the Elk-dog band arrived, in which to evaluate the situation. Then it must be discussed in the council.

By the evening of the council, the entire tribe was in an uproar. Entire bands were taking sides. Oddly, some of those who were most involved were not even of the Elk-dog band.

The Mountain band, feeling the family connection because of Willow's marriage, were solidly behind Owl's claim to the office. That was as it should be.

The Red Rocks band, long close associates of the Elk-dogs, were a smaller band, and had no medicine man of their own. A strong pressure group had formed among the Red Rocks to persuade Owl to join them.

Most militant of all were the Eastern band. For reasons not yet clear to Many Robes, the Eastern band were so incensed that, almost to a man, they were ready to go to war over the situation. True, they had no medicine man, and it was apparent that they wished Owl to join them. But even this did not explain the militant attitude of righteous indignation that pervaded the group.

Many Robes had consulted with the other medicine men of the tribe. There were two. One, of the Mountain band, was a practitioner of the Night Prophet persuasion. He was old, and his specialty was the foretelling of the future by means of visions. He mumbled and chanted and scattered small bones and sticks on his painted medicine skin. Then he shook his head. Bad things were ahead, he predicted. He could not see clearly, because the vision was clouded by the power of other medicines.

The medicine man of the Northern band, a respected practitioner of buffalo medicine, disqualified himself from any decision on the basis of his profession. It would not be appropriate, he insisted, to pass judgment on another's skill.

Neither of these would be of any help at all, Many Robes thought. Both, in effect, wished to remain completely outside the conflict. It was wise, he realized. He could see their concern for their own prestige. What if they should back the wrong faction? Still, the old chief sighed, it made his job no easier.

He talked with Heads Off, who was very depressed over the whole affair, and felt somehow responsible for the trouble in his band. Many Robes tried to reassure him. Such things are no one's fault, he observed. They merely happen. Had he but have known, the real-chief actually forestalled even more trouble with this conversation. Heads Off had been on the verge of offering to resign as chief of the Elk-dogs. The encouragement of this conversation made him reject this possibility, at least for the present.

Many Robes felt that it would be best for him not to talk directly to the two principals in the dispute, but he discreetly inquired as to their actions.

Owl, he learned, was staying with his wife's people among the Mountain band. He was attempting to remain inconspicuous. It was said on good authority that he wished to avoid trouble, and that he had offered to accept the place of medicine man to the Red Rocks band. However, his wife and his family would not hear of such a thing. The matter must be decided in council.

Aiee, it falls on me again, thought Many Robes.

The other principal, Two Dogs, now asking to be called White Buffalo, was in haughty seclusion. Any effort to talk to him was rebuffed. He was privately seeking a vision, his helpers stated, as he had been told by his medicine.

Many Robes was upset by this news. There was no way to be sure whether some sort of trick would be attempted.

In all his years, he had never approached a session of the Big Council with such apprehension. He watched the preparation of the council fire for a time, and then turned to dress and prepare himself for the ceremony. With tempers running high, it was apparent that whatever happened would have far-reaching effects for the People.

Many Robes was tired. He found himself wishing that he were younger. Then perhaps he would have more confidence in his ability to handle this situation.

33

The **Big Council** proved to be nearly all that Many Robes had dreaded.

No sooner had Sun Boy's torch dipped beyond the rim of the world, than the People began to gather. Never had a Big Council been so well attended. By the time the council fire had been lighted and all the chiefs and sub-chiefs seated in their appointed places, there was a buzz of nervous excitement in the air.

To most of the onlookers it seemed an interminable amount of time that was occupied in the ritual smoke and the opening statements of the band chiefs. Heads Off, of the Elk-dogs, was very brief in his opening speech. He acknowledged the unexpected return of his son, Owl, who had been considered dead, but scarcely mentioned the matter that was uppermost in everyone's mind.

Many Robes himself introduced the matter of two medicine men in conflict for the authority of the white buffalo cape, and then the council began to deteriorate rapidly.

Two Dogs arrived, late, at precisely this time. To the shocked amazement of all, he was wearing the precious white cape, usually reserved for buffalo ceremonies. It was a flagrant abuse of authority, in the minds of many. He made a dramatic entrance, and sat before the council in almost haughty contempt.

Several people asked to speak before the council, and each was recognized. Many Robes intended that everyone should have his opportunity to be heard. People testified that Owl had completed his apprenticeship before his abduction. And, did not his very return indicate the strength of his medicine? White Bear, chief of the Red Rocks band, formally offered the endorsement of his band, and the invitation to join them.

No one spoke in behalf of Two Dogs. He obviously considered his claim to the position to be so valid that defense was beneath his dignity. And, it could not fail to impress the onlookers that after all, he was wearing the traditional white cape.

The council seemed to be moving toward an uneventful vote, which Many Robes felt would probably go to the son of Heads Off. He was uneasy about it, however. There was a lot of feeling, and he detected a certain undercurrent in favor of Two Dogs. It could not be denied that Heads Off had originally been an outsider, and his son, Owl, was of mixed blood.

The real-chief saw no incongruity in this situation. Heads Off was one of the most respected of the band chiefs, with strong elk-dog medicine to his credit. Yet, there were some who still resented him as not of the People.

A woman asked to speak, and was recognized by Many Robes. He somehow overlooked the fact that this might be the spark that would set the whole council ablaze. The young mother brought her child forward, a rosy-cheeked youngster of perhaps six summers. He was a smiling,

healthy child. Suddenly Many Robes realized that the
woman was emotionally relating a very stirring experience. This child, she was practically shouting, had been
snatched from the very jaws of death by the greatest medicine man the People had ever known.

"With no medicine things, even, and with a borrowed
drum, he did this thing!"

The young woman's husband rose to stand beside her.
Many Robes recognized one of the rising young sub-chiefs
of the Eastern band. Ah, so this explained the preoccupation of that group with the dispute. The real-chief had not
been aware of the child's illness. The young chief was almost shouting now. He reiterated all that his wife had said,
and then, before Many Robes realized the gravity of the
moment, he suddenly threw forth a challenge. Thrusting
his lance into the ground, he continued his speech.

"—and I am ready to meet in combat any who deny the
strength and wisdom of this medicine man!"

A roar of approval rose from the young warriors behind him. The Eastern band was, indeed, ready to fight,
the real-chief realized. Apparently he had underestimated
the strength of their resolve.

An angry mutter rose from near the seat of Two Dogs.
One of his "helpers" sprang to his feet, shouting angrily,
and weapons flashed. Voices rose, and the entire situation
seemed about to erupt into violence.

Many Robes clapped his hands sharply, and the noise
subsided somewhat.

"There will be no fighting among the People!" he ordered firmly. Devoutly, he hoped his command would be
respected. He did his utmost to appear as if he expected
it. There had once been a time, he reflected, when he
could have commanded these young hotheads without
question. If necessary, Many Robes could once have enforced the command with sheer physical superiority.

"You will be seated!" It was an order, not a request,

and the young warriors took their places. The real-chief breathed more easily. Things were temporarily under control.

Many Robes was noted not only for his past physical prowess, but for his ability to think rapidly in time of crisis. He now evaluated this situation quickly.

One thing was certain. The matter must not be allowed to come to a vote of the council tonight. Either way the vote went, the losing faction would overreact, and there would be bloodshed. That would cast a shadow over the coming Sun Dance that could never be erased from the history of the People.

It must not happen. If he could keep the situation undecided, there was still hope for a compromise. So, the vote must not come, with tempers running so high. The real-chief could think of only one way to prevent a call for the vote, so he rapidly took action.

"Tonight, we must all seek a vision," he announced blandly. "The council is dismissed. We will meet again tomorrow night."

The People were dumbfounded. This was a development unforeseen by anyone. The crowd began to scatter, with some grumbling, but it was clear that the threat had passed.

Many Robes rose and made his way back to his lodge. He wished he were as confident as he tried to appear. He had gained a little time, but that was all. He still had no clear idea of his next move. Certainly, he must seek a vision.

34

Coyote left the council with an amused smile on his face. How adept had been the handling of the thing by the real-chief! He had taken the only possible action, that of dismissing the council. How neatly had he drawn the fangs of a poisonous situation!

But, the problem still remained. Coyote was glad that the responsibility was not his. Sooner or later, Many Robes must act. It must be with extreme care, to prevent serious damage to the People. This was only one of the reasons Coyote had never had any aspirations to leadership positions. From outside the critical center of things, one could see more clearly. And, if the truth were known, Coyote rather enjoyed the possibility of gently managing the course of things. He could drop a word here, a gentle nudge there, to move the ponderous workings of the council, or the thoughts of an individual mind. Coyote enjoyed the manipulation involved.

Just now, he circulated around the camp, listening to the buzz and chatter. Things were quieting slowly. Some small groups still hotly debated the issues, but it appeared to be just talk.

A group of young people had brought a drum, and around the remains of the council fire they had started a social dance. More wood was brought, and more people joined in the songs and dances. Good, thought Coyote. That will give them something to do besides make trouble.

He was waiting until later, until things quieted somewhat, to make his move. There was no hurry. Coyote knew that Many Robes would not be sleeping during this night. Strange, on the night the real-chief must dream a vision, that he would be unable to sleep because of that intense need. Coyote chuckled softly to himself.

It was well past the middle of the time of darkness when he at last approached the lodge of the real-chief. The dancers had dwindled to a few hardy souls, and most of the People had retired. He tapped softly on the skin of the real-chief's lodge.

"Who is it?"

"I am Coyote, my chief, of the Elk-dog band. I would speak with you."

Many Robes, lying sleepless on his pallet, rose to an elbow and sighed in the darkness. Coyote. Yes, he remembered. The fat little warrior, said to be among the most shrewd of the Elk-dog band. Old Hump Ribs, their previous chief, now long dead, had valued Coyote's wisdom and advice. Perhaps he should listen to the man. And, was he not, Many Robes recalled, related somehow to the family of Heads Off?

"In a moment. We will talk outside. It is too hot in here."

He was, he now realized, sweating in his sleeping robes, only partly from the temperature.

The cool air felt good on his face as the two men walked

down along the stream, and Coyote began to outline his
ideas. Soon the real-chief was listening enthusiastically.
This little man might easily have hit upon the solution.
Many Robes nodded from time to time, asked a question
here and there, and started to lay his plans.

At one point they returned to the lodge of the real-
chief, and a young woman was sent on a secret errand.

Soon the two were joined by a very sleepy individual,
the medicine man of the Northern band. At first he was
grumpy and irritable, but after listening a short while, became as enthusiastic as his chief.

They talked a long while, planning the course of action. Coyote, after listening for a time, took his leave and
quietly slipped back to his lodge. He was pleased with the
night's work.

Tensions mounted through the day, and again, the
meeting of the big council was sure to become a critical
time. People began to gather before darkness fell.

Owl was reminded of that which occurs when one
places a stone from the stream bed in a fire. The water
spirits in the stone engage in combat with the fire spirits,
and at some unexpected moment a mighty explosion tears
the stone apart.

On the previous night, Many Robes had dragged
out the formalities of the ceremony, but now he almost rushed through them. The pipe was passed and returned to its ceremonial case by the real-chief's pipe
bearer. Now the council could begin. All eyes were on
Many Robes as he cleared his throat and spoke with
confidence.

"We have had before us the matter of two medicine
men. Which is the real one? Who has the true medicine?"

He paused a moment for effect, as a murmur ran through
the crowd.

"I have seen a vision."

More muttering, in approval now. At last the problem would be resolved.

"In my vision, I was made to see that we who know nothing of buffalo medicine must not be the ones who decide. It must rest on the skill of each medicine man, and on the strength of his medicine."

A restless murmur arose. What did the chief mean by this pronouncement? He raised a hand for silence, and continued.

"Who knows better which medicine is best," he went on, "than the buffalo himself? We will let the buffalo decide."

Now there was puzzled confusion. The thought seemed good, but what did it mean? Many Robes was continuing.

"Plans will go ahead for the Sun Dance. Meanwhile, there will be no hunting of buffalo. This will be enforced by the warrior societies. No one must disturb the buffalo!"

He looked around the circle to make certain this edict was understood. It was an important part of the plan. There were nods of understanding, and Many Robes felt that it would be so. The People, by tradition, were expected to abide by the rules of the tribe.

"Now at a time to be announced, the skill of the medicine men will be tried. This will not be a public contest. Its conditions will not be known until the day arrives. Then all will be told."

All else in the council was now anticlimactic. It is doubtful if anyone remembered any of the announcements or decisions. The arrangements for the Sun Dance were discussed, but that would be routine.

Owl was puzzled. What could be the meaning of Many Robes' strange vision and pronouncement "—let the buffalo decide"?

In the darkness of the back rows, Coyote chuckled quietly to himself. Things were moving well.

Meanwhile, trusted scouts had been dispatched in all directions to locate and observe the buffalo. The plan depended on the presence of a large herd in an undisturbed state. When that necessary ingredient was available, the test would begin.

35

The tense situation was relieved somewhat. There was the excitement of the Sun Dance to become involved in, and the People seemed to feel that if a solution was in the offing, no further action was necessary. They were willing to wait on the course of events.

The Sun Dance was to last six days, and the formal announcements were begun by the crier the morning after the Big Council. With face paint carefully applied, he circled the entire camp repeatedly, blowing his eagle-bone whistle and announcing the event. This ritual continued for three days, and then the Dance proper began.

This most important event of the People's year was designed to give thanks for return of the sun, the grass, and the buffalo. There were also vows and patriotic sacrifices and a general theme of rejuvenation. The curative and restorative powers of the Sun Dance were well known to be effective. Elderly limbs, warmed by the excitement of the occasion, did seem to lose some of their arthritic limitations and actually become younger.

The ceremonies continued nonstop, day and night, exhausted dancers being replaced by others as they retired from the medicine lodge.

But behind all the excitement of the occasion was the question of the medicine men. What had been the vision of Many Robes? How could the buffalo "decide," as the real-chief had said? There were rumors, of course. It was known that there were scouts on a secret mission. It must be concerned with the buffalo, since hunting was forbidden. Just why was not clear, but the taboo was strictly obeyed.

Owl idled around the camp. His emotions were a strange mixture. There was joy at his return to the People and the festival excitement of the Sun Dance. At the same time there was guilt because he was not accomplishing anything. *Aiee,* how many seasons had passed since he was neither pushed to learn nor to survive! He scarcely knew how to use the free time with which he found himself. However, he had a willing companion to help him in any use of time. Willow almost embarrassed him with her devotion. It was a delight to be with her, and the two had never yet exhausted the surprise and thrill of just being in each other's company.

The big question, of course, was still the resolution of the problem concerning the false medicine man. Together the two tried to decide what form the contest would take. Owl had no qualms as to his own skill in whatever test was presented. He had some doubts about the skills of Two Dogs. There was no way of knowing how much the other had learned from old White Buffalo. And, of course, Two Dogs did possess the white cape. Was it possible, Owl wondered, to steal the medicine of another? Would he, in a contest, be in combat against the medicine of his own teacher? That would be a grim situation. How could he compete against the medicine of one so wise and old as White Buffalo?

These were the emotions that alternately affected Owl as he slept, ate, danced, played with little Red Bird, or spent long hours in company with Willow. When the message finally came that would relieve the tension, it came as a surprise.

It was on the evening of the third day of the Sun Dance that a messenger came from the real-chief, with instructions. Owl stepped outside his father-in-law's lodge to talk with the warrior. Owl must be ready to travel at dawn. He might take anything he wished that would pertain to his buffalo medicine. Two people would be permitted to accompany him as assistants, and they must carry food for three days.

The medicine part was easy, thought Owl. He had nothing except the medicine pouch around his neck. If he were to work with the buffalo within the herd, he would need a calfskin, but that was easily borrowed.

Of course he had no assistants, either. He must choose two to go with him for moral support in the undertaking. They must believe in him, and have the strength of spirit to enhance his medicine.

Of his first choice there could be no question. It must be Willow. They had shared so much, good and bad, and since their reunion they had become all but inseparable. He stated his intention, and the messenger nodded in assent.

The second choice was more difficult. Owl would have selected his father, Heads Off. He had always seemed a mountain of strength to the boy as he grew up. This time, however, because of the conflict, Heads Off would be disqualified. It would be better not to request him than to be refused.

"For my other assistant I choose Coyote, my grandfather."

Again, the messenger nodded acceptance. He pointed to a distant hill.

"You will meet the real-chief at the top of that hill when Sun Boy shows his torch."

Turning, the warrior strode swiftly away.

There would be little sleep this night. He must inform his father, borrow horses, and oh, yes, the calfskin. Rapidly he outlined the situation to Willow and her parents. The girl immediately started to assemble supplies, while her father offered a horse for her to ride. Owl would ride the claybank mare. He hurried away to ask his grandfather's cooperation.

Coyote was delighted, but managed to hold his enthusiasm in check. Yes, he said, he would be proud to go. He would furnish his own horse.

Owl hurried on to his parents' lodge and poured out the story. It was here that he borrowed the needed calfskin. Tall One embraced him and admonished him to be careful, and he kissed her and reassured her.

"Mother, this is only my duty as a medicine man! I have been taught well!"

He tossed the yellow-furred calfskin cape over his shoulder and stepped out into the night. Heads Off accompanied him for a way, walking in silence. The distant beat of the drums and the muffled chant of songs came from the medicine lodge. There was a slight acrid odor of dust in the air, mingled with smoke from cooking fires and the heavy damp smell of the dew.

"My son, I wish I could be of more help to you," Heads Off spoke at last. "I have not been there when you needed me."

They walked on in silence. Owl knew that, though it was true, there had been reasons. It seemed half a lifetime since he had apprenticed himself to the profession of the medicine man. Actually, he had himself felt some guilt at neglecting his parents.

If Owl had only known, his father was twisted by an even more complex set of emotions. Heads Off, with the return of his son, had been thinking often of his own parents far away. Only now did he begin to feel to some extent the suffering his father and mother must have experienced. They must have long since become reconciled to the fact that their only son's bones lay scattered on the wide prairies of New Spain.

Now his own son, Owl, had returned. Heads Off took great pride in his son's achievements, but as always found words difficult.

"I know you will do well," he spoke hesitatingly. "May all your medicine be strong."

Heads Off grasped the hand of his son in the ritual handclasp of the People, and turned quickly away into the night. There was so much he had wished to say, but could not express.

Owl stood for a moment, also wishing for the ability to communicate. Sometimes, he pondered, there are no words to say things of the heart. He hoped that his father understood. It meant a great deal to him that Heads off had wished him good medicine.

36

The eastern rim of the world was just becoming muddy gray with the false dawn as the three rode out of camp. There was a sleepy muffled thump of the drum from the medicine lodge, as a few dancers held forth. More would arrive soon for the increased activity of the day.

They picked their way across the prairie in the general direction of the appointed hilltop. Small birds, waking to the growing light, darted from in front of them. A distant coyote cried to his mate on an opposite bluff, and from a wooded ravine came the hollow call of the great owl.

The riders had traveled some distance before they saw three other horsemen in front of them. The advancing daylight allowed identification of Two Dogs and his two assistants. It could be seen that all three were heavily armed, with both club and lance. One also had a bow slung across his back.

Owl suddenly realized that he might have committed a

grave error. Two Dogs was ready for a violent showdown. If it came to a fight, here were three well-armed fighting men. Owl's party, by contrast, consisted only of himself, his wife, and his grandfather. He tried not to think of their extreme vulnerability, and did not speak of it. He knew that the others were thinking similar thoughts.

Why, oh, why had he been so stupid, Owl asked himself. He had been thinking in terms of a contest of medicines. Two Dogs was obviously prepared to establish his authority by force. Owl regretted leading his wife and grandfather into this crisis. How much better to have brought his brother Eagle and one of the other Elk-dog men.

He glanced at Willow, riding beside him. Her grim, tight-lipped smile showed that she followed his thoughts. The friends of Two Dogs might find that they had underestimated this situation. Owl thought of the demise of Many Wives. That was a side to the nature of this slim woman of which Two Dogs was unaware.

Owl looked at his grandfather, riding to his left. Coyote, who was certainly not the best of riders, was bouncing along comfortably, enjoying the swaying motion of the horse. His eyes were half closed and he hummed a little song as he enjoyed the dawn and the waking of the world. He appeared completely unaware of any problem on the entire earth, but Owl was not deceived. From past experience he knew that Coyote had missed not one thing. It was simply not yet time to worry.

Nevertheless, Owl slowed their pace. It would be poor judgment indeed to ride up behind heavily armed adversaries. His own lance and the short knives of his companions would be poor defense if the trio turned to attack.

A great blue heron lifted heavily from a small creek ahead, and once airborne became the most graceful of creatures. Daytime birds were becoming more active, and the air was alive with their songs. Furry puffs of fog hung in patches along the stream or drifted among the scattered trees. It was a day that showed promise of quiet beauty, and to Owl this was a good sign.

Nevertheless, it was with a great sense of relief that he saw ahead of them the waiting riders on the hilltop. Many Robes himself sat majestically on his horse, flanked by two other men. Owl relaxed somewhat. It was encouraging that the real-chief considered this confrontation important enough to preside over personally. It was also reassuring to see that he was accompanied by two trusted warriors of the Northern band. Apparently Many Robes had anticipated the possibility of violence, and was prepared to back any decision by force if necessary. This would insure fair play. Owl's basic optimism was restored.

The real-chief nodded a greeting.

"It is a good day," he announced to the group. "Let us travel."

Turning his horse, the real-chief started at a smart walk across the prairie. Owl, scarcely thinking about it, noted that they were headed in a northwesterly direction. Many Robes rode with one of his warriors at each elbow. Owl's party spread out to the left and the group of Two Dogs to the right. The strangely assorted group scattered nine abreast across the plain.

It was an ideal day to travel. The assorted flowers of the prairie were at their finest, scattering scraps of white, pink, yellow, and indigo in pleasantly unexpected places. The yellow-breasted meadowlarks sang in constant chorus, and a red-tailed hawk circled on effortless wings above them. For Owl this time of teeming life on the prairie was truly his homecoming. Even the tension of the situation could not stifle the exhilaration he felt at being home.

At noon they reached a clear spring, and Many Robes called a rest stop. Owl, though in good physical condition, was stiff from the long period on the horse. There had been only short stops occasionally, and it was good to walk and stretch the legs. How much more uncomfortable the travel must be for the aging real-chief, and for Coyote, no athlete at best.

Those two older men sat apart, sharing a smoke without speaking. Owl noticed that one of Two Dogs' friends hovered nearby, trusting no one. Two Dogs himself sat haughtily to one side, apparently considering it beneath his dignity to acknowledge the presence of the others.

When everyone had rested, drunk, and eaten lightly from the supplies of food, Many Robes gave the signal to depart. The grazing elk-dogs were assembled, and the party remounted.

The rate of travel was again a brisk walk. From the attitude of the warriors of the Northern band, Owl deduced that they would reach some sort of destination by the time of darkness. This theory was reinforced when one of the men rode ahead and returned in a time to confer with his chief. He pointed ahead, and the direction of travel was altered slightly. Soon they were met by another warrior, who talked at length with Many Robes, and remained with the party, acting as a guide.

Shortly before Sun Boy slipped beyond the world's edge, they arrived in a little valley with water and grass, well sheltered from view.

"We will camp here," announced the real-chief. "There will be no fires. But first, we will all go very quietly to the top of the hill to look."

They dismounted stiffly, and the scout led them on foot to the broken rocky crest of the hill above them, cautioning quiet.

Owl peered around the edge of a limestone outcrop. Spread out over the plain before them was a magnificent herd of buffalo, dotting the prairie as far as the eye could see. The setting sun cast a golden yellow haze on the slight dust raised by the creatures. Here and there there was a glint of the fading rays on a polished black horn. An occasional cow called for her calf as the herd began to settle for the night.

Owl saw that it was good.

37

After a restless night the contest of medicines was to begin. Owl was happy that he had had a warm and loving companion to share his robe through the long hours of darkness. Not merely physical was the strength he derived from this girl. Willow, from the time he first saw her as a prisoner long ago, had had the ability to bring out the best in him.

They had whispered long through the night, mostly about nothings. However, when the time came to face the morning and all the stresses of the day, Owl felt that he was at his best. His slim wife had again managed to make him feel that he was the strongest, most astute, and most capable man alive.

The group went again to the crest of the hill and Many Robes outlined the conditions of the contest.

"You will see," he pointed, "a ridge to the west, with several little canyons."

Yes, it was apparent, several fingerlike projections from the main ridge formed a series of similar canyons between, each opening onto the level plain before them. Owl began to see the way the contest would take place.

"There are two canyons better than the rest." The chief pointed.

Yes, it was true. Near the center of the formation, two of the blind-end canyons were very similar in shape. Both had narrow entrances, but opened out inside.

Prior to the use of elk-dogs in hunting, this would have been an extremely important type of formation. For more reasons than a dog has hairs, the People had hunted buffalo in similar areas. The medicine man had used such a canyon as a trap, enticing the animals within the natural walls. Then the entrance had been blocked by hunters, who could more easily kill the buffalo attempting to pass them at the narrow spot.

Now, the old skills were to be used again. Owl thought briefly of how he had resented the gruff old medicine man's insistence that he learn. Now he was thankful.

"You will each use one canyon."

Owl quickly evaluated the two best sites. One had a slightly narrower neck, harder to make the animals enter, but perhaps better grass inside. The most northerly of the two canyons, he decided, would be the most desirable.

"I will cast the plum stones to choose which canyon you will use."

Many Robes took forth a small pouch and shook out five plum seeds. One side of each was painted red. He shook them in his cupped palms and prepared to roll them upon a flat stone.

"Owl, you are reds!" He tossed the objects, and they bounced and skittered to a stop. Two showed the painted surface, three the natural color of the seed. Many Robes turned to Two Dogs.

"Yours is the choice."

Of course, Two Dogs chose the best of the two canyons. No matter, thought Owl. There was little difference anyway.

"Now," Many Robes was speaking again, "you may start at any point on this side. You will put as many buffalo as you can into your canyon." He paused long enough to thrust a spear upright into the ground. "When the shadow of my spear falls upon this rock," he pointed, "the contest is over. Whoever has the most buffalo has the strongest medicine and will become White Buffalo! We will watch from here." His tone, slightly more firm than necessary, said plainly that the real-chief would be on the watch for trickery.

Owl took the calfskin cape from his grandfather and adjusted it carefully around his shoulders and head. He must look as much as possible like one of the yellowish calves playing in the meadow below. He clasped his grandfather's hand and embraced Willow. Then he turned and started down the ridge.

After a few hundred paces Owl shrugged into his crouch and turned directly into the herd. It was slow. It must be. His actions must be in direct mimicry of those of a calf. Faster motion would startle the great beasts, and they must remain undisturbed at all costs.

He threaded through the herd, apparently aimlessly, but working toward the opening of the blind canyon assigned to him. He gradually began to get the feel of the mood of the herd. He was "inside their heads," as old White Buffalo had expressed it. Their mood was quiet and peaceful. The herd had been grazing quietly in the area for some time, and there still appeared adequate grass. The situation was ideal for such a test as now presented, Owl believed.

He worked among the animals for a time until he was sure of the animals' attitude, and then began his task. He noticed a pair of calves cavorting playfully near the canyon's mouth, and joined them in play. The two calves, enticed by their strange playmate, drew out away from the herd, until finally a cow called a warning.

Now was a critical moment. Owl kicked up his heels and scampered toward the opening, followed by the calves. The cow's bellow became more insistent, and she came lumbering after her errant offspring. The dam of the other calf, now noticing something amiss, rose and trotted after. A large bull which had been in their company followed ponderously, and a yearling calf joined the procession. Good! The first few were most important. A variety of ages and sexes would more easily encourage others to join the little band.

Owl led the group well inside and into choice lush grass before he slipped away and returned to the open prairie. He wondered how Two Dogs was faring. Had his opponent actually spent the hours and days necessary to do this sort of work? The uneasy thought crossed his mind that perhaps Two Dogs was even better than he. And, so much depended on luck. A chance false move, a startled animal beginning to run, and all would be over.

He looked in the direction of Two Dogs' area of effort, but could see nothing beyond the hundreds of slowly moving animals.

He selected a new calf that appeared to want to play, and began to maneuver it to the edge of the herd. The cow followed, with another yearling, probably her last year's calf. Owl was disappointed to spend so much time for only three animals, but they moved to join his previous nucleus, and he returned to the herd again. He was uneasy. There was a limit to the number of times the buffalo would tolerate his movement through the herd before they became uneasy.

But, as he approached the main herd again, he noticed a couple of coyotes trotting among the scattered animals at the edge. There were always coyotes among the herds, and sometimes the big prairie wolves, too. The animals circled, waiting, hoping for a sick or injured calf. This kept the strength of the breeding herd at a good level, Owl knew, by the elimination of weaker individuals. He watched the pair of coyotes, wondering if in some way he could use their presence.

Suddenly the nearest of the animals turned, directly facing him, and sat on its haunches. The head cocked whimsically to one side, and clear yellow eyes stared straight into his. There was something familiar about the pose, and the facial expression of the coyote. Even then, it took him a moment to recognize his medicine animal.

As soon as Owl made recognition, the coyote turned and trotted away, but the meaning of the visit was clear. The day was to be good. His medicine animal was with him.

38

True to his expectation, the next sortie into the herd netted twelve more animals. Those inside the canyon were beginning to bed down comfortably, and the new-comers joined them, completely undisturbed. Owl wondered about how much time might be left, and cast a glance at Sun Boy's torch. He was unable to tell. He must simply continue to work buffalo until notified that the trial was over, he supposed. It bothered him a little. The main herd might become restless, and his smaller group would attempt to rejoin them if a general move began.

He turned again into the herd, stepping cautiously around an irritable-looking old bull. Suddenly he noticed a subtle change in the mood of the animals. There was nothing at first that he could quite identify. It was merely a quiet unrest, an uneasiness of mind. Owl would have missed it altogether, he thought, if he had not been inside their heads. He stood still, trying to identify the source of the feeling. A yearling bull blundered past him, curiously seeking the source of the same unrest.

Owl was undecided. He could withdraw quietly and stand guard at the entrance to his trap to prevent the buffalo already there from leaving. That was probably the most sensible course, but what if Two Dogs had more animals gathered? Could he take that risk? Or, would he risk more to continue working the herd? He glanced around, hoping to see his medicine coyote again, but the creature was nowhere in sight.

With a feeling a little like panic, Owl wondered what was causing the growing restlessness in the herd. Several of the younger animals were moving in the same direction, ears pricked forward in curiosity and wonder. He decided to return to his gathered herd. The animals were becoming too restless to work with now.

His direction of progress was with the general drift of the disturbed buffalo. Then, ahead, Owl caught a glimpse of what must be the inciting factor. A handful of yearling calves were gathered around a misshapen light-colored object that moved in a strange unnatural fashion. At first he thought it was one of the big wolves. They were sometimes very light gray in color, but the movements were not appropriate. The creature moved like a buffalo, but was much smaller, and almost white in color.

The thought crossed his mind that here was a young white buffalo. If he could only entice that individual into his trap, he would prove that he was the possessor of the greatest of all buffalo medicine. The one animal would prove beyond a doubt who was more fit to inherit the title.

Owl moved to a position where he could better see the animal. Other buffalo shifted and shuffled, and dust rose, blocking his view. He must not lose sight of the sacred animal. He moved closer.

Then, with a shock, Owl realized the truth. The figure was that of a man. Two Dogs! He was actually wearing the precious white cape of the medicine man, handed down through so many generations. What a fool, thought Owl, to risk the sacred object in the milling herd.

He had no way of knowing whether Two Dogs had started the contest wearing the white cape, or had changed at some time since. Regardless, it was a fool-hardy thing to do. The unusual appearance would be more likely to alarm the herd than quiet them. Could it be that Two Dogs believed the cape's medicine alone would protect him?

The other man moved closer, and Owl changed position to avoid the shifting of the restless animals. He lost sight of Two Dogs for a moment, and when he saw him again, the white-caped figure was closer yet.

At last Owl realized what was happening. The other man was maneuvering the disturbed animals to present a threat to his opponent. Three young bulls snorted and wheeled, almost running over him. Skillfully, Owl skipped aside, alert to the next danger.

Owl now realized that Two Dogs had never intended this to be a legitimate contest. The other expected to take the life of his challenger in any way he could. Owl was completely unarmed, but knew that Two Dogs would be carrying, at the very least, a concealed knife. He must avoid both his old enemy and the shifting, nervous buffalo, now beginning to snort with alarm and jump skittishly about. The fool could get them both killed, he now feared. He tried to retreat, but the crouching figure in the white cape moved closer, stepping among the animals. He did possess a certain amount of skill, Owl saw, but he was careless.

When the decisive event finally came, it was so sudden that even Owl was surprised. Two Dogs, intent on approaching his enemy, failed to observe the rudiments of his medicine. He allowed himself to come between an old cow and her small calf. The calf gave a short bleat of alarm, and the mother wheeled to defense.

White Buffalo had made much of this point. One must

never, never be caught between a cow and her calf. If a cow threatens, put her calf in front of you. Two Dogs, having forgotten these basics in the passion of the moment, now stood completely defenseless. He tried to jump, but the massive head of the angry cow swept him aside as she drove to reach her terrified calf.

Two Dogs, now off balance, was flung against one of the big herd bulls. The animal, already irritated and on the alert by the bleating of the calf, now perceived this strange creature as the threat to the herd. The great head swung, and a polished black horn pierced soft under parts of the intruder. In the space of a heartbeat the head swung upward, tossing Two Dogs high over the backs of the animals. Not until then did he scream. It was a long, shrill death scream, throwing nearby animals into a running frenzy.

Owl saw the frantically flopping white-robed figure strike the rump of a young cow, and she lurched forward in a panic. The others began to run, and an earth-shaking rumble began to spread as hundreds of startled buffalo started to stampede.

Before he quite realized it, Owl was running, too. All sense of direction was gone. There was only one, that of the herd. In a moment he managed to clear his thoughts, trying to create some sort of plan as he ran.

His long hours and days of training with the buffalo had put one thing foremost. When working with buffalo, one must appear to be a calf. He must move, act, walk, even smell like a calf. Now, he thought grimly, he must run like a calf. He was already sprinting as fast as he could, trying to match the speed of the herd. Fortunately, he found himself in a group of cows and calves. The small animals were just a bit slower, and the cows were holding back a trifle to wait for the youngsters. Owl saw a calf running, pressing close against the flank of the mother. Perhaps he could imitate. He leaned toward an animal on his right, and grasped a handful of thick curly hair at the shoulder. By holding

tightly, he was partly carried along and was able to maintain more nearly the speed of the animals. The cow tossed
her head at him, but was more concerned with running.

Owl's lungs were burning, his legs tiring rapidly. Soon
he must let go and when he did, he would instantly be
trampled by the animals running behind. This thought
alone kept him moving, running for life.

An animal just ahead stumbled and rolled, then another, and something struck him just below the left knee.
He realized that this portion of the herd must have run
into a strip of limestone rimrock. A large square boulder
loomed ahead and he half fell and scrambled behind it,
dragging his injured leg.

It seemed a long time that the thunder of the herd continued. Animals fell, were injured, scrambled up and continued to run, limping. He must have been near the edge of the
herd when the panic started, he knew, or the push of the animals behind would have crushed those who fell. A buffalo
stumbled over Owl's very boulder, almost landed on top of
him where he crouched, and rolled to its feet to run on.
Thick dust choked him, he could not see, or breathe, and he
had to stifle the urge to jump to his feet and run in a panic.

It was nearly nightfall before the herd began to thin, and
complete dark before the choking dust settled to allow him
to look around. He tried to stand, and found that he could
not use his left leg. Frustrated, he wrapped himself in his
calfskin for warmth and settled down for the night.

It was probably just as well, he decided, that he must stay
here. He had no clear idea of direction anyway. Perhaps he
could see more in the morning.

39

Intermittently through the night, Owl slept fit-
fully, woke, and slept again. He was chilly and stiff. Each
time he wakened he discovered areas of soreness of which
he had been unaware. His left leg throbbed painfully.

He was certain the bone was not broken, because, to
the best of his memory, he had run several steps before falling. Maybe it was the smaller bone. Gingerly
he touched the puffy area below his knee. At very least,
there was a lot of internal bleeding about the area. He
shifted uncomfortably.

The distant rumble of the thundering buffalo herd had
faded and was inaudible now. The dust was settling, and
Owl could begin to see the sky and the outline of distant
hills. He began to orient himself by the stars. There he saw
the Seven Hunters, the last two pointing the way to their
lodge at the real-star. He had been badly disoriented, he
now saw. The herd must have run in a southerly direction.

With this in mind, he looked in the direction of the camp. There, on the distant crest of the ridge, twinkled a signal fire. It was good. At least, the rest of the party had survived. Some of them, anyway. He had confidence in the self-reliance of Willow, Coyote, and the real-chief, and apparently the main herd had not turned in their direction.

With something of a surprise, he realized that they must now think him dead. There was little likelihood of anyone's surviving the stampede. They had lighted the fire in the slim hope that one or the other of the medicine men might still be alive. Owl realized that the fire might as well be many days' travel away. He could not travel well enough to reach it tonight anyway. Neither did he have any means to light a signal fire of his own.

Owl coughed heavily, burning his lungs and bringing up large quantities of salty-tasting phlegm. In the dark he wondered if it were blood. He turned on his side and drifted again into fitful sleep.

The dream wakened him. It was a dream that would haunt him many times in the future. He was running, all his muscles aching in protest, and hanging suspended, high in the air above him, was Two Dogs. The other seemed to float there, face distorted and mouth open in a death scream. The edges of the sacred white buffalo cape fluttered in the wind.

Owl woke with a start, sweating and anxious. The distant signal fire still burned. He hoped that they would come looking for him at daylight. His thoughts turned to his dream and to the death of Two Dogs. He was certain of the man's death. It was only a question whether he had died from being gored and tossed. It was possible, Owl supposed, that the other had lived long enough to realize that he was being chopped to pieces by a thousand sharp-edged hooves.

And, what of the white cape? It, too, must be torn to scraps by the trampling herd, and scattered by the prairie winds. Owl was still unable to comprehend the loss of the cape, one of the most sacred medicine objects of the People. He sank into sleep again, his every muscle sore and aching.

Daylight presented a desolate scene. The great herd was gone, as surely as if it had never existed. Scattered here and there were individual animals, crippled or dead, trampled by the frenzied thousands. Vultures were gathering, circling on non-moving wings.

Owl turned to look at the ridge where the signal fire had burned. A thin line of smoke rose straight upward. Good. They had not given up on the chance of his survival, and were maintaining the signal fire. He pulled his aching body to a standing position, coughing painfully. He saw with satisfaction that his sputum was black from the dust, rather than bloody.

He stood, weak and swaying, trying to decide his next move. He doubted his ability to cross the intervening prairie. If he could only light a fire to attract their attention. But he had no fire sticks. Given time, he might contrive some. His primary concern was that the group on the distant ridge would give him up for dead and leave without him. He had no idea at all whether he would be able to move about enough to survive and find the People.

He decided to attempt to move toward the wisp of smoke. The distance would be less than half a sun's travel for a man able to walk. Owl, however, rapidly discovered that his pace would be much slower. Every jarring, limping step sent pain crashing into the base of his skull, and exertion also initiated paroxysms of coughing. In a short while he realized that it would take him several days' travel to reach the ridge. Meanwhile, he had no food. He sank down in the grass, aching in every muscle and joint.

Thirst, too, was beginning to make itself felt. After resting, Owl decided to try to make his way to the stream. No matter what the next day or two might bring, he must have water. Painfully, he limped and crawled to the creek, stopping frequently to rest. He drank deeply, and sat back against a tree, too exhausted to move further.

He sat, becoming more discouraged as time passed. Was the power of his medicine gone? Had it been so closely tied to the medicine of White Buffalo that it had been trampled in the dust with the sacred cape? He fingered the medicine pouch around his neck and wondered.

Hoofbeats roused him from his dejected reverie. A rider on an elk-dog was passing along the ridge of the hill above him. Owl recognized one of the warriors who had accompanied Many Robes. The man looked constantly in all directions as he rode. Owl realized they were searching for him.

Weakly, he tried to shout, but the thick phlegm in his throat prevented the sound. Frantically, he cleared his throat, coughed, and managed a weak croak. The warrior did not hear, and continued to ride on. Three times Owl tried to call out, before the man turned and saw his feeble wave. Then he came clattering recklessly down the slope, shouting to others who were out of sight beyond the hill. There was a great deal of respect and deference in the warrior's attitude as he attempted to make Owl more comfortable and offered him food. Very slowly, Owl began to realize that his survival from the stampede would be regarded as the greatest of medicines.

Other hoofbeats were clattering down the hillside, and in a moment he was tenderly engulfed in the soft embrace of his wife. Her grateful tears were moistening his neck, and over her shoulder he saw Many Robes and Coyote picking their way across the slope.

The real-chief swung down and walked toward him, a trace of a smile on his stern visage.

"*Ah-koh*, White Buffalo," the chief spoke. "It is well with you?"

Owl thought a long time before answering. He had not

given thought since the stampede to the fact that the office and title of White Buffalo would be his. Now it seemed an anticlimax. Weakly, he cleared his throat.

"My chief," he managed to whisper, "that day is ended. The white cape is gone. I will be called only Owl, medicine man of the People."

Many Robes nodded in understanding. Owl began to relax, as the others prepared to make camp. Someone was kindling a fire.

Willow still held him closely yet gently, inquiring about his various injuries. Owl smiled and touched her glossy hair. Here in her arms, he knew, was his strongest medicine of all.